ZOO'D

DATE DUE

Prairie du

ISBN: 0615730582
ISBN-13: 978-0615730585

For our mom, Mary Jac, who taught us that life was an adventure and if you weren't having fun, then you needed to change your course.

ACKNOWLEDGMENTS

The Nardini Sisters would like to thank their families for their continuing support. A special shout out and thank you to their brother, Craig, who markets them every chance he gets. Much thanks to our editor, Lou Belcher, and our junior editor Jessica Lowell. Thank you to our niece, Marina, who has an amazing eye for catching last minute mistakes.

Gina would like thank her husband, Scott and her friends who have provided support. Gina would also like to thank all her students who continually asked for the sequel to *The Underwear Dare*. Here it is, guys. Thanks for the motivation! One more thanks goes to Miss Elizabeth Rowe, who diligently read the first forty pages of a very rough draft and caught many errors.

Lisa would like to thank all her friends, especially Renae who still reads everything she's ever written. Many thanks to all the Delta flight attendants who continuously show interest in her writing. Special thanks to Matt, for his encouragement and ability to always bring a smile to her face. And to Dean…still riding on her coat tails.

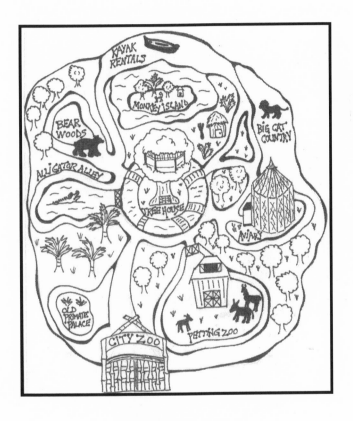

Map of City Zoo

CHAPTER 1

"Ed-die! Ed-die!" The chanting started.

I was the only one not joining in. Eddie, my crazy step-brother, was in the throes of blowing a gigantic bubble. He wanted to set a new world's record for biggest bubble and since bubblegum was not allowed in middle school, he knew he'd have to set his record on the school bus. Never mind it wasn't allowed on the bus either.

"Ed-die! Ed-die!" The chanting was getting louder as the bubble got bigger. My friend Paul nudged me to join in. I did, even though part of me was a little bit jealous and the other part of me was a little worried about getting into trouble.

"POP!" In a flash, the gooey mess exploded like a thousand sprays of silly-string with

1

most of it landing on Marina, Chelsea and Bria.

"Eeeewww!" was all I heard from the girls as they scrambled to remove the pink sticky globs from their hair.

"I'm sorry, I'm sorry," Eddie said to them over and over, but they ignored him.

I swear I heard Marina mumble, "Idiot."

"Josh, did you see that?" Eddie asked me. I was busy looking at Manny and Paul's diorama that had shattered in a million pieces on the bus floor.

I nodded in disbelief. The bus looked like a giant bubblegum bomb had exploded.

"I was so close. I think I need more gum." Eddie's bubblegum obsession started right after our little sister was born. He even kept A.B.C., **A**lready **B**een **C**hewed, gum in our freezer. It was gross!

As we were getting off the bus, the driver stopped Eddie, "Edward, a minute please."

Eddie froze.

"See you later, Eddie," I said and hurried to homeroom.

The principal's office waiting room. That is where I sat. On the most uncomfortable chair on the planet with the most uncomfortable feeling in my gut. It was all Eddie's fault, of this I was sure. Look at him there. Sitting comfortably and as cool as a cucumber. The principal's office never rattled him. I guess if you spend as much time in there as he has, the terror wears off.

"I know you think this is my fault," he said, "but I can assure you Josh, I've done nothing wrong today."

"Really?" I said.

"Really," he replied.

"Bubblegum," was all I said.

"Oh, yeah, right," he chuckled. "That was really funny."

Eddie was right. It really was funny, but not so funny now.

"I just don't know why I'm here," I said.

"Oh, about that, when the bus driver asked me where I got the gum, and I told her it was yours."

"What?"

"Well, it was the truth."

"Dang it Eddie! I could, I could…" I was interrupted by the sweet smell of strawberries as Marina, Chelsea and Bria strolled into the principal's waiting room. It was obvious that they had tried to remove the strawberry gum from their hair, but had just made it worse. Marina's long brown hair stood straight out, Chelsea's curly black hair looked like two swirly horns and Bria was sporting a blonde Mohawk.

"You!" Marina pointed at Eddie. "You are so in trouble now!"

Neither one of us could answer, we were laughing so hard at her hair. This made her angrier and she sat down in a huff. Chelsea and Bria imitated her to let us know they were angry, too.

Our two best friends, Paul and Manny, entered the office with their prized diorama in pieces. They sat down and shot Eddie daggers.

"What happened to your diorama?" Eddie asked them.

"Like you don't know," Paul spat.

"Honestly, I don't."

"When your bubble popped, it was so loud that Manny accidentally dropped our diorama on the floor," Paul said.

"No way? It was loud, wasn't it?" Eddie boasted. "I mean, I'm sorry, I didn't mean for that to happen."

Principal Hamilton's door opened and she poked her head out. One of her eyebrows was raised higher than the other in a questioning look. She glanced at the girls' hair, then at the busted diorama and then at Eddie and me.

Her other eyebrow caught up with the higher one. A look of surprise was on her face.

"Alright, inside all of you," she said as we followed her into the office.

We squished onto the benches and chairs in her office and she sat behind her desk. Her office was neat and tidy and was full of certificates all over the walls. It was kind of intimidating.

Principal Hamilton's clear blue eyes honed in on Eddie. "Is there something you need to tell me Edward?" she asked. I knew why she'd asked him first. Trouble kind of hung around Eddie. He might as well wear a sign around his neck that said *trouble*. Come to think of it, he did have a t-shirt in the fourth grade that said, *Here Comes Trouble*. I wondered what happened to it.

"Yes, there is. I must confess," Eddie said and paused, then continued, "I confess, that you look very pretty today."

"Uh-huh. I see. Well, I'm sure you know why you are all here." She glanced around the room, stopping at Eddie. "Edward, I believe you owe these girls an apology."

"I'm sorry you guys. I really didn't mean to get gum all over you," Eddie said.

The girls just glared at him.

"Ladies, go see Mr. Jeffries. He might have something in the cooking lab that can get that bubblegum out of your hair. If anyone can get it out, he can."

The girls left, but not without giving Eddie a final glare. He acted like everything was okay and said, "Alright, see you guys in language arts. I'm glad we could clear this up."

Principal Hamilton cleared her throat. "Edward and Josh, what do you think we should do about Paul and Manny's diorama?"

Josh? Why was she including me in the destruction? Oh yeah, my gum. Not fair. Not fair at all. Thanks Eddie.

"Well, we could explain to their social studies teacher that it was our fault and we could help them rebuild it after school," Eddie said and added, "I'm really sorry my expert bubble blowing ability ended up making you drop your diorama."

"That sounds reasonable. Do you agree Josh?" Principal Hamilton asked.

"Um, yeah. I'm sorry, too, that Eddie's the bubble master and it seems trouble follows him wherever he goes," I said even though I didn't think I should be held responsible. I sounded pathetic.

"That's okay with me," Manny said. Of course, he would agree quickly. Manny's easy

6

going and he's one of my best friends. Best friends don't stay mad long.

"Paul, is this acceptable to you?" Principal Hamilton asked.

"Yeah, but it has to look just as good as it did before," Paul grumbled.

"It'll look better!" Eddie said and I knew he was right. Eddie was an amazing artist. The diorama was themed *From Harvest to Table*, and to be honest, it didn't look that good before the gum catastrophe.

"You two are excused," she said to Paul and Manny.

"Now boys, what do you think your consequence for this action should be?"

"I really feel like I learned my lesson already," Eddie said.

"Try again," she muttered.

"Excuse me, Ms. Hamilton, I don't really think I should be held responsible for Eddie's actions," I said with all the courage I could muster, which wasn't a lot.

"Interesting," she replied and took a deep breath. "Josh, I was wondering if you could tell me our school policy on gum?"

"It's not allowed," I mumbled.

"Of course it isn't. Do you know why?"

"Kids blow bubbles and it gets everywhere. Also, we stick it under our desks."

"Um-hum. So you know you broke the rule by supplying gum to a fellow student. Do you still think that you shouldn't shoulder some of the blame?"

"Honestly? No. I know I shouldn't have brought gum to school. But I wasn't the one who blew the bubble."

"I see you still have much to learn, Josh," she said disappointedly.

I didn't care. I was so sick of Eddie always dragging me into trouble with him. Sure it was a fun ride along the way, but when we got to the end, boy did we pay. I had never even been grounded before Eddie became my step-brother a year ago. Still, I was smart enough to see I wasn't going to get out of this without some major butt kissing. So I said, "Maybe we could write a report on how important it is to keep our school gum-free?"

I could write a report in ten minutes flat. Not to brag, but I'm a straight-A student and this seemed like the easiest way out of a sticky situation, no pun intended.

"I do think it's very important to keep our school gum-free. Gum is a sticky business and no good has ever come of it."

"Some gum helps clean your teeth," Eddie added in his most innocent voice.

"I see. And how many cavities have you had, Edward?" Ms. Hamilton asked.

It was a trap. I knew it, but couldn't warn him. Principal Hamilton was just too smart for Eddie.

"Three," he answered.

"Obviously, you do not chew the kind that cleans you teeth. Do you know what you will be cleaning during your lunch period?"

"My teeth?" he whispered.

"The bus. It's a mess. You two will work as a team to clean it up. And I hope I don't hear about anymore bubbles, Edward, or anymore gum, Josh. You two will report to Mr. Foley, the head custodian to let him know you will need some cleaning supplies, and then go to your first class. You are excused."

"Why'd you have to say you got the gum from me?" I asked Eddie as we walked to see the custodian. "Now we're both in trouble."

"Because I knew I'd get in trouble and it is more fun having punishment with a friend," Eddie answered.

"A true friend wouldn't tattle."

"A brother would always have your back, even when you had to clean the bus."

I couldn't argue with that. Eddie was my brother. Well, my step-brother, but he hated when I added the "step" in front of the word "brother" so I just stopped doing it. It was useless to argue with him. He always seemed to say something to bring you over to his side. He didn't used to be like that. He used to bully you to get his way. He changed last year when his mom married my dad. We became friends somehow, despite the fact that he had picked on me mercilessly since kindergarten. Still, I wasn't ready to let him off the hook yet.

"You know Eddie, since you've been my brother, I've been grounded seven times, had two detentions and one suspension."

"Hey, you're right! Wow. That's cool!"

"Ah, no it's not. You always get me in trouble!"

"Josh, you're looking at it the wrong way."

"What other way could there be?"

"My way. See, since *you've* been my *brother*, I've only been grounded seven times this year. That's excellent! Last year I was grounded a total of fourteen times. You helped me cut my average in half! Not to mention I had six, yes, six detentions the year before. That's even, well, more than half! You're good for me!"

"Well, you're not good for me," I said but regretted it right after I said it when I saw the look on his face.

"Oh," was all he said.

CHAPTER 2

After we got the Gum-Out, a bunch of rags, and a couple of paint scrapers from Mr. Foley for later, we went to our language arts class. Mrs. Kairys, our super cool teacher, was asking if any of us had experience naming a baby. Eddie's hand shot up instantly as he took his seat.

"Yes, Eddie?" she asked.

"I named my baby sister Alwilda," he said proudly.

"Oh, interesting…" she said but looked confused.

"I know. I'm really good at naming babies. Would you like me to name yours?" he said referring to the fact that she was pregnant.

"That's really kind, but I think my husband and I can manage. We like Hannah because it is a palindrome."

"That's the name I chose!" I shouted before I realized it.

"Good to know we're on the same page, Josh," she answered.

"I meant, that was the name I chose for my baby sister, but Eddie won the dare and…"

After I said, "the dare" all eyes turned to me. It was like I was starring in a movie. It got super quiet. Everyone knew about how Eddie and I used dares or bets to solve our disagreements. It got us into some hot water last year in the fifth grade, when one of our dares went a bit too far. Let's just say it involved me and Eddie running across the cafetorium in our underwear during lunch. We were legendary for that dare, but the dare to name our baby sister was not common knowledge. Although I knew it would be soon, now that I blabbed.

"What I meant to say is Hannah is a cool name. I like how it's a palindrome; you know, how it's spelled the same backward or forward," I rattled on, which I tend to do when I get nervous. That, and I turn as red as a beet, which I was right now. But Mrs. Kairys was so cool, she continued like nothing happened.

"Anyway, there is a contest to name the new patas monkey at our local zoo, so after we do some team research on the patas monkey, each team will get to submit one name. Now students, I want you to really do your best because the team that wins will get to spend the night at the zoo!"

Cheers and hollers from all of us. Spending the night at the zoo would be awesome!

So do we get to stay in the Tree House?" Eddie asked without waiting to be called on.

"I don't know, I suppose so. I think that's the only place for overnight guests to stay," Mrs. Kairys said.

"Too cool, I heard they just added zip-lines over the zoo," Paul couldn't contain his excitement.

"That's true. My dad told me all about it," Manny added.

Mrs. Kairys looked worried. "I had no idea the zoo was so progressive."

We all looked at each other. *What did progressive mean?* We all shrugged our shoulders. Mrs. Kairys realized we didn't know the word.

"Does anyone know the definition of progressive?"

Eddie raised his hand.

"Yes, Eddie."

"It means the animals are very dangerous because they are so pro-aggressive and if you fall off the zip-line, you will get eaten."

"No, no. Anyone else?"

"My dad has insurance called Progressive. Does that mean the zoo needs insurance because the animals might eat us if we fall off one of the zip-lines?" Bria asked.

"First of all, no one is going to get eaten by the animals at the zoo. I'm sure all the zip-lines are very safe." Mrs. Kairys sat down at her desk. She wiped her forehead with the back of her hand. She looked tired.

"Now where was I? Oh yes, progressive. It means to always move forward and make use of the most modern ideas, like adding a zip-line. Our City Zoo was the first to provide kayaking as a way to explore the zoo, too."

We did have the best zoo. I really wanted to spend the night there. My thoughts were interrupted by Mrs. Kairys.

"Okay, I'll give you a couple minutes to break up into teams. There will be three teams with seven students each. Each team must have boys and girls together and each member of the team will be responsible for researching one key fact about the patas monkey."

Eddie and I instantly sought out our two best friends, Manny and Paul. They seemed to be over the gum incident. Manny is like that, though. Nothing ever ruffles his feathers for long. Even though he grew a few inches over the summer, he's still the shortest boy in our class; however, he's the fastest runner in the school. No one can catch Manny. Paul is tall and blonde and lanky. He's the only kid taller than Eddie. He didn't used to be, but he grew over the summer too, and passed Eddie.

"We need some girls," Paul said. "Let's ask Marina, she's the smartest girl and Josh, since you're the smartest boy, we/ will have a great team."

"I don't think they want to be around me and Eddie right now," I said.

"Hey, Bria do you want to join us?" Manny said. I knew he'd asked her because he had a crush on her, which was sort of funny because she was the tallest girl in our class and he was the shortest boy. She was short last year and kinda chubby, but she'd had a growth spurt over the summer, too, like Paul.

"Sure," Bria said and walked over. Her long blonde hair was now gum free and fashioned into a braid down her back. It looked pretty but a little greasy.

"Wow, you smell really great!" Manny said, "What is that?"

"Oh, it's peanut butter. Mr. Jeffries used peanut butter to get the gum out of our hair and then he braided our hair to make it look better. He's way into fashion. It's kinda funny because you can still smell the strawberry gum and now it's mixed with the peanut butter. I smell like a PB&J."

"Peanut butter takes gum out of stuff, who knew?" Eddie said to no one in particular.

Chelsea joined us next. She was super cool and really pretty. She had brown skin and black hair, which was twisted into two braids right now, courtesy of Mr. Jeffries, the family and consumer finance teacher. I kind of had a small crush on Chelsea, but I kept my distance because she still seemed a little mad. But, she was nothing compared to the steam engine that was making her way towards us now.

"Traitors!" Marina hissed to Chelsea and Bria.

"Oh, Marina. Just get over it. It was kinda funny," Bria said.

Marina plopped noisily into an empty seat and sulked. She played with the end of her new French braid.

We scooted our desks together and waited for the next set of instructions.

"Here is a list of facts you need to answer about the patas monkey." Mrs. Kairys said as she handed each team a research sheet. "Take a few minutes to decide who will get what fact and then we'll go to the media center."

Marina, done sulking now that there was a job to do, grabbed the sheet right away and designated herself as our leader. She was kind of bossy that way.

"Okay, I'll read the facts and then we can pick who gets what." She read: "*Habitat, eating habits, social hierarchy, newborn care, lifespan, physical description, and interesting facts.*"

"I'll take *physical description*," Manny said and Marina wrote his name down on the worksheet.

"Aw, that's what I wanted," Paul said.

"Oh, okay, you can have it." Manny's good nature shone through once again.

Marina erased Manny's name and wrote down Paul's.

"No, that's okay. I just wanted it because it sounded easy. You can have it," Paul said.

Marina erased Paul's name and carefully rewrote Manny's.

"That's why I wanted it, but really, you can have it," Manny insisted.

Marina erased Manny's name and tore a hole clean through the paper. "Enough!" she yelled. "Look what you two made me do. I hate holey paper, it's so imperfect. Manny, go get us a new sheet. Paul, pick something else, Manny called *physical characteristics* first."

Manny scrambled to Mrs. Kairys' desk.

"Well, Paul?" Marina said

"I'm too scared to remember the other six categories," Paul said.

"How about *lifespan*? That one's even easier than *physical characteristics*."

"Yeah, that sounds good," he agreed.

"I'll take *social hierarchy* because that's probably the hardest one," Marina said writing her name down on the crisp, new research sheet Manny provided. In the end, Bria ended up with *eating habits*, Chelsea got *habitat*, Eddie got *interesting facts* and somehow I got *newborn care*.

We sat in the media center, at a large kidney bean shaped table to review the information we had gathered from books, magazines and the internet. Marina had loads and loads of index cards covered with notes, Bria had one sentence on her index card, Chelsea had one full index card, Manny and Paul had one index card between them and I had a full index card front and back. Eddie ran up to the group and plopped in the last chair.

"I got some great stuff! Really super cool!" he said.

"Let's all state one thing we learned while researching, and we will keep going in a circle until all our facts have been shared," Marina said. "I'll start. As you know, my category was *social hierarchy*. Here is fact one…"

"Dang, you could have said two facts by now," Eddie interrupted and I had to agree.

"Anyway…as I was saying, patas monkeys usually live in groups," she stated.

"Patas monkeys are reddish-brown in color with some white and grey hair, and they have super long legs like a greyhound for running really fast," Manny said. "That's all I have."

"Really? We've been researching for half an hour," Marina said.

Manny looked crestfallen.

"I found something really interesting about their appearance," Eddie added.

"Cool, thanks Eddie," Manny said.

"You're welcome. I found a website that said that the monkey's white mustache makes it look like an old British military officer. So I came up with a name for the baby monkey, it's…"

"Hang on, we were all supposed to work together to come up with a name," Marina said.

"Well, if you would let me finish, you'll see my plan involves everyone's help. You see, I thought the name Chortles would be a cute name for a baby monkey..."

"That's good, Eddie," I interrupted. "It's friendly and makes it sound like the monkey likes to laugh."

"That's what I thought! Who sees a monkey laughing and doesn't laugh, too? Except that mean one who threw that banana at you a couple of years ago, Josh."

"Only because you threw it at him first," I answered. "I'm pretty sure that he was aiming it at you."

"Then that monkey had terrible aim and should have practiced more. Anyway, if we name him Chortles, then we could each give him a name based on each letter. What's that called again?" he asked.

"Acronym," Marina and I answered in perfect unison.

"Yeah, that's it. An acronym. Let's give him an acronym using the research we found."

"Eddie that's brilliant!" Marina said and I swear I saw Eddie blush a little.

"Hey, I get it! Since my category is *physical characteristics*, I'll start his name with the letter "C" for Colonel, since he looks like a British soldier," Manny said.

"That's brilliant, too," Marina added.

Eddie looked a little deflated to lose his brilliant title so quickly to Manny.

"Next is "H." Any ideas?" Marina asked enthusiastically.

"Huffingpants," Paul said and giggled to himself.

"That doesn't tie back to our research at all," Marina said.

"Yeah, but it's funny," Paul said.

"I guess so, but if we're going to use an acronym, then we need to do it right," she insisted. She wrote the word CHORTLES really big on a piece of paper with a fat, black marker. She wrote it vertically, so we could fill in the letters with ease. "Now let's brainstorm. We can use what we've learned and apply it to the letters."

We spent a good fifteen minutes checking over our research to come up with the perfect descriptive terms for CHORTLES. Finally, after lots of debate and team work, we agreed on the following:

C = *Colonel, because their mustaches and scowls make them look like colonels*

H = *Hamstery, because they can hold food in their cheeks like a hamster*

O= *Omnivorous, because they eat insects and vegetables*

R = *Racer, because they are the fastest monkey*

T = *Treenap, because they sleep in trees*

L = *Lionel, because lions like to eat them*

E = *Ever-ready, because they always have a scout on lookout for danger*

S = *Scruffers, because their long red and gray fur is scruffy*

"So, the long version is: Colonel Hamstery Omnivorous Racer Treenap Lionel Ever-ready Scruffers. C.H.O.R.T.L.E.S. for short," Marina said, and we all agreed.

CHAPTER 3

"Come on, Eddie, we're gonna be late." I looked at the clock.

Eddie was jamming tons of stuff into the world's largest backpack. "I'm almost ready," he declared.

I had packed my bag earlier that day. I still couldn't believe our team won the "Name the Patas Monkey" contest. It was like we won the lottery. I couldn't wait to get there.

"It's just one night at the zoo. How much stuff do you really need?" I eyed my backpack on the bed, it was barely full.

"See, that's the difference between you and me. I'm packing for the *what-ifs* and you're packing for the *no-ifs*."

"What? I don't know what that means." I sat down next to my backpack.

"Always be prepared, just like a boy scout." Eddie told me as he threw some firecrackers and a long rope into the backpack, along with other gadgets I had never seen before.

"You were never a boy scout." I reminded him.

"That's true, but it doesn't mean I don't believe in their motto. Also, I believe in *Semper Paratus* or *Always Ready*. That's from the U.S. Coast Guard."

"You were never in the Coast Guard."

"Fine, but do you know how many shows I have watched about search and rescue and how to survive the wild?"

I could only imagine. Eddie was legendary for watching television and then remembering everything he ever saw. However, this didn't apply to his school work. He was barely an average student. He was diagnosed as being a visual learner in school. That simply meant he learned better by watching instead of reading or just plain listening.

"Eddie, you do realize we will be sleeping in a tree house built by the zoo, not really outdoors. Plus, all the animals are in cages, not running wild. Nothing is going to happen."

"You're right. Not on my watch!" he said and struggled to zip up the overstuffed backpack. He then donned a safari vest and began filling the pockets with more stuff.

"Boys, it's time to leave!" My step-mom, Allie, shouted from downstairs.

I slung my backpack over my left shoulder. Eddie's was so big and heavy he had to carry it with two hands down the stairs.

"One last thing," Eddie said to me, "My secret weapon."

I watched as Eddie opened up the freezer door. There were rows and rows of different colored wads of used chewing gum. Eddie pried off several wads and put them in one of his vest pockets.

"That's disgusting," I said.

"Yeah, a little." He smiled.

There is an amazing freedom one feels when riding the bus away from school on a school day. We were off to the zoo for our overnight trip. Just our little group of seven plus three teachers: Mrs. Kairys, Mr. Kairys (he teaches math and is her husband) and Ms. Freiberger, the meanest substitute since Ms. Sniedendorf from our elementary school years.

The teachers were sitting in the front and talking as usual. We were in the back and Eddie was in the middle of telling a cool story. This one was about how our baby sister got her name. The bus windows were down. The wind whipped through our hair and made it hard to hear so we all leaned into the aisle from our seats.

"So then I say to Josh that I am thinking about a series of dares to see who gets to pick our sister's name. He wanted Hannah, not bad really, but my baby sister deserved a name worthy of a queen. So, I chose Alwilda," he bragged.

"That certainly is different," Marina said.

"Sure is! It's the name of a beautiful, pirate princess from long ago."

"Wait, how'd you get your parents to agree to let you name your kid sister?" Paul asked.

"Josh came up with a way," Eddie said as all eyes turned to me.

"It was easy," I said, "We just told them it would make us feel like we were part of the whole process and all; that we really wanted to be a close family, and they bought it."

"So what were the dares?" Paul asked.

"Well, the first dare was a piece of cake, literally," I said.

"You mean figuratively," Marina said.

"No, I mean literally a piece of cake." *Did Marina spend her nights reading the dictionary?*

"You mean the first dare was an actual a piece of cake?" she asked.

"Not a piece, no. The whole cake!" Eddie laughed. "It was a cake eating contest. See, my mom had just baked a cake: chocolate with chocolate frosting. Then, she made the fatal error of running some errands and leaving us alone with the cake. Since I got to pick the first dare because I won Rock, Paper, Scissors, I picked cake. I dared Josh that I could eat half of the cake faster than he could. I'm sure you can guess who won."

"Obviously," Marina said.

"If obviously means I won, then you are right," Eddie boasted.

"Didn't you get in trouble eating all that cake?" Manny asked.

"Manny, this is important so listen good," Eddie said.

Manny and everyone else leaned in close to hear Eddie's words of wisdom. Eddie cleared his throat, "Sometimes you have to take a chance in life, even if you know that the consequences might be bad, if it means winning."

"That's a terrible thing to say!" Marina said.

"Is it? Sure my mom was mad. And yeah, I had a really bad stomach ache for a whole day. I got grounded, too. But I won the bet and no one got hurt. Except my stomach, it hurt really bad. And now, when I see chocolate cake, well, I just can't eat it anymore." Eddie looked sick just thinking about it.

"It's awesome, because chocolate is Allie's favorite flavor and she makes it all the time. I get extra because Eddie doesn't like it anymore. So who do you think really won that dare?" I asked knowingly while nodding my head and raising an eyebrow.

"Anyway, the next dare wasn't as cool," Eddie said.

"He only says that because I got to pick that one. For my dare we each had to design and build our own kites. Whoever flew their kite the highest won," I said. "Of course, I used my math skills and designed a precise flying machine. My kite flew to the clouds."

"And what about your kite, Eddie?" Manny asked.

"It didn't fly as high as Josh's did, but it was way cooler than his was. I painted a really scary flying dragon on it with fire spewing out of its mouth!" he said.

"That is cool!" Manny said and everyone else agreed. Eddie's art skills were renowned.

"Thing is, all that paint made it heavy and it didn't fly well. I did get it off the ground, but not for long."

"Yeah, and into the closest tree." I laughed.

"So you guys were tied. What was the final dare?" Chelsea asked.

All eyes were on me. "The final dare was one that involved our neighbor, Ms. Jenkins. See, Ms. Jenkins has a spazzy, little poodle that always gets out of her collar and runs around. But this time, she ran around Ms. Jenkins feet and tripped her really bad. She broke her ankle," I said.

"Yeah, then she hired me and Josh to mow her lawn and take care of her shrubs and flowers on account of her being all lame and stuff," Eddie added. "The money wasn't bad and we always divided up the yard. So, this gave me an idea; the next time we had to work in her yard we would ask her real innocent like, which side of her yard looked better. Whichever side she chose, then that was the winner of the final dare."

"That's it? That's kind of boring," Marina said.

"Is it? Well, you don't have much of an imagination then because this turned out to be the most fun and best dare of them all!" Eddie said.

"He's right. It was. We could do whatever we wanted to her yard. She could barely leave her house. Ms. Jenkins had rows and rows of shrubs and stuff. I thought it would be cool to shape all her shrubs into the geometric forms we learned in math class. I shaped her shrubs into pyramids, cubes, rectangular prisms and spheres. The spheres were the hardest."

Oohs and aahs from my classmates. "I know, cool, huh?"

"What did you do, Eddie?" Chelsea asked.

"Well, first I thought about forms too. Then I thought, what does Ms. Jenkins love more than anything else?"

"What?" They all said in unison.

"Keep it down, back there." Ms. Freiberger turned around to yell at us.

Eddie lowered his voice and continued, "Gigi, her poodle."

Our friends erupted into laughter, even I couldn't contain myself. Eddie was the best storyteller ever.

Freiberger turned back to us again with her finger on her lips and told us to keep it down or else. What a grumpy grumpleton!

Eddie continued in a low voice, "I shaped all the shrubs on my side into poodle heads and tails. She loved it. I won!"

"Yeah, she loved it so much that Eddie had to reshape all the shrubs on my side into poodle heads and tails, too. She wanted her yard to match on both sides," I said, still laughing.

"True, I didn't think that through and had to do double the work but that's how Alwilda got her name."

Gigi Shaped Bushes

CHAPTER 4

The bus doors hissed as they closed behind us and paradise lay in front of us. City Zoo was hands down the coolest zoo on the planet! I looked at the bamboo entrance gates; they were so tribal and Tiki-like. I knew we were going to have a complete blast. Just then, Mrs. Kairys let out a terrible wail.

"What's wrong?" Mr. Kairys said rushing to her side.

"It's the baby, I think it's time!" she yelled.

"But it's one whole month early," he said panicking.

"Try telling the baby that." She panted.

We stared as Mr. Kairys loaded Mrs. Kairys back onto the bus. "We are going to the nearest hospital," he ordered the bus driver and then he stuck his head out of the door,

"Can you manage the kids without us?" he asked Freiberger.

"Seven kids? I can do that with my eyes closed," she said and grinned creepily as the Kairys sped away.

Something about that grin made me nervous. Just then, a chubby guy wearing a zoo uniform shuffled over to greet us. He was in need of a shave; his clothes looked like they had never seen an iron, and he wore a dirty baseball cap that read, "City Zoo." He smelled like a hamster cage that needed to be cleaned.

"Hi kids," he said in a very friendly tone. "My name is Horace Oscar Gandenthal, but everyone calls me HOG. I'll be your guide for your overnight adventure. Our zoo manager was going to take care of you all, but, he had a family emergency, so I got the call. Well, not really. They actually called six other zoo workers before me, but they were all busy. So I volunteered! Now don't you worry, because I know everything there is to know about this zoo. I've done just about every job here too, from maintenance to feeding and caring for the animals. Heck, I just finished cleaning the iguana cage a few minutes ago!"

That explained the smell.

"Now if you'll just follow me, we will head to the Tree House where you can stow your things, and then we'll take a complete tour of the zoo."

We all followed Hog through the cool bamboo gates.

"Now you'll do well to remember that the zoo is set up like a wheel. The Tree House is smack dab in the middle of the zoo or wheel. The different sections of the zoo are the spokes, each leading back to the Tree House."

We all started walking to the Tree House. Even though it was a school day, there were still families at the zoo. Hog explained that they closed at five and after that we would have the zoo all to ourselves. When we got to the Tree House, Eddie let out a low whistle.

"Wow," was all I said. It was amazing! It was hands down the biggest tree house I had ever seen. I knew it was a man-made tree, but it looked so real. The trunk of the tree was about the size of our cafetorium, and it had to be a hundred feet tall. Above my head, I saw cool balconies. I imagined the views were spectacular!

"Pretty impressive, huh? Wait until you see the inside of the lobby," he said.

We followed him through a double set of bamboo doors into the heart of the tree.

"Whoa, check this out! It looks like we're inside a tree!" Paul said as he rubbed his hands along the walls.

The lobby was super cool. It had carpet that looked like actual grass. Wicker chairs, couches and tables were set up where people could relax and talk. Right now, a lot of moms and dads lounged around as their kids explored the area. I couldn't wait for everyone to leave so we could have the tree house all to ourselves. There was a gift shop, a first aid station, and administrative offices.

"Josh, check out that safari hat," Eddie said as he pointed to the window of the gift shop. "It has a light on it! I've gotta have it! And there's a really cool canteen that matches it!"

"Strictly impulse buys, Eddie. They have no practical use," I said.

"What do you mean?"

"We don't live in a desert or down a mine shaft. We have faucets and light switches."

"They could be for the what-ifs, my friend. The what-ifs…," he trailed off.

I shrugged. Eddie could be so dramatic.

The girls squealed when they saw a giant stuffed monkey in the window. It was huge! Easily the size of a small adult. I bet Alwilda would love it. She would fit perfectly into its lap. I pictured her all curled up asleep on the giant stuffed animal. Maybe I could buy it for her? I looked at the price tag, $100.00. Wow. Maybe not.

Hog continued his tour. "Now, there are two ways to get up to the second and third floors. You can take the elevator, which we will do today because of your luggage, or you can take the stairs."

Hog piled us into the elevator, which was covered in some kind of cool woven grass wallpaper. We exited onto the second floor which contained sleeping quarters and class-rooms.

"Now, you will notice that we have two rooms for sleeping. Girls on one side, boys on the other," he said.

We entered our room and threw our back-packs on the beds. It was a pretty cool room with rows of cots, some hooks and bamboo shelves for storage, and a bathroom. But the best part was the far wall. It was made entirely of glass from the top of the ceiling to the bottom of the floor. You could see half the zoo through it. We all ran for it and pressed our noses against the glass.

"Look at that cool pond!" Paul said.

"That is Alligator Alley. We have twenty alligators that call it home," Hog said.

"Whoa, I think I see one moving!" Paul said.

"Probably not. It's very warm today and alligators like to lie still and bask in the sun. I saw it on a show about reptiles called, *Modern Dinosaurs Among Us,*" Eddie said.

"Okay boys, I'll give you all a few minutes to freshen up, and then I'd like you to report to the Canopy Café on the third floor where I'll show you something truly amazing," Hog said and left.

After he left, we immediately got our phones out and started taking pictures, which we then posted instantly.

"I can't believe we get to stay in this room with no grown-ups!" Manny said.

"I know! It will be the best, most ultimate sleepover ever! Don't you agree, Eddie?" I asked.

"It is pretty cool and all. I've always wanted a tree house, but it's important not to let your guard down," he answered.

"What do you mean?" Manny asked concerned.

"Well, Manny, there's a lot of jungle out there and the animals are feral. Feral means "wild" in explorer speak," Eddie said making quotation marks in the air with his fingers.

"I'd hate for one of them to get loose; it could be disastrous."

"Come on, Eddie. It's a zoo with a man-made jungle. It's not real. The animals are in cages. Sturdy, strong cages. That would never happen," I said.

"Not real, huh Josh? Those alligators look real to me," he said as he pointed to the glass. "Remember it's about the *what-ifs*, not the *no-ifs*," he said.

"Not-no, what-ifs, what?" Paul asked as he wrinkled his brow.

"Exactly," was all Eddie said.

I just shook my head and smiled. Eddie had watched one too many nature-gone-awry movies. "Come on guys, let's check out the girls' room."

The girls' room was almost as cool as ours. It overlooked a giant bird cage where tons of birds were flying around.

"Whoa, what's that?" Manny asked.

"Humph! Has your teacher been neglectful of your vocabulary? It's called an *aviary*," Ms. Freiberger said.

The Aviary was a massive structure with steel beams that climbed from the ground to the sky. But there were no walls. Where the walls should have been, there was netting instead to keep the birds in. It was full of all kinds of birds imaginable. It was very impressive.

Together, we headed to the top floor and entered the Canopy Café. The room had big glass windows all the way around it so you could see the entire zoo while you dined. Because the zoo was still open, a lot of people were still there. I made a mental note to sneak back up there tonight to check it out when it was empty. Hog waved us over to a large round table.

"Okay, now that you're all here, we'll go over today's itinerary," Hog said as we all sipped on orange juice and nibbled on donuts. "We'll start at the Petting Zoo, and then make our way counter-clockwise to the Aviary and Big Cat Country. We'll take a quick break for some lunch and then we'll go kayaking around Monkey Island. After that, I'll give you a brief lecture and demonstration on how to handle wild animals. Then we'll finish the tour with Bear Woods and Alligator Alley. For dinner, we'll come back up here after hours and I'll round you up some grub."

"Is he a cowboy now?" I whispered under my breath and Eddie giggled.

Chelsea raised her hand and asked, "Can we hold some of the smaller animals during the demonstration?"

"Well, young lady, wild animals are nothing to trifle with. You must remember to always be on your guard."

"That's what I said!" Eddie exclaimed.

"And you're right, son. I can't tell you how many times I've been bitten by the animals here."

"But the animals that you're using for the demonstration, they are all in cages, right?" Manny asked.

"Sure they are," he smiled, "Unless they get out."

"Excuse me, sir," Ms. Freiberger spoke up, "I'm sure you would not let the animals out around these children, would you?"

"No ma'am! Not intentionally, I mean that hasn't happened in a long while anyway…" he trailed off clearly not wanting to talk about it anymore.

I wondered if he was a little forgetful, as in maybe he forgot to close the cages before. He seemed a bit flaky and he tried too hard to act like he knew it all.

"Now for that special surprise! Are you ready, amigos?" he said as we eagerly followed him out to the balcony that encircled the Canopy Café. "This was the special thing that I wanted to show you," he said as he stepped onto a wooden platform that jutted out from the balcony. It over-looked Monkey Island. Two very long cables were attached to the end of the platform and disappeared just over the island in a continuous diagonal drop. They had weird harnesses dangling from them.

"This is a zip-line. You fasten yourself into the harness and you 'zip' down to Monkey Island," he explained.

"Whoa, that's cool!" Manny said and we all agreed.

"Do you stop on Monkey Island?" Marina asked. "That doesn't seem very safe."

"Actually you zip over the island and land on the far shore where we keep the kayaks. We also have a zip-line over Alligator Alley. It's not open to the public yet, but later to-night you can all give it a whirl."

"Why isn't it open yet?" Marina pried.

"Did someone fall into the alligator pond?" Eddie asked knowingly.

Hog cough and acted like he hadn't heard Eddie. Maybe Eddie had guessed right.

CHAPTER 5

Our first stop on the tour was the Petting Zoo. The girls squealed with delight and ran straight inside. Us boys hung back and took our time like we were too cool.

"Oh, my gosh! Look at the cute donkey!" Marina said, as she scratched an old gray donkey behind his ears. "Quick, take a picture for me," she said to Bria.

Bria took the picture and then decided she wanted one with a cute, brown pony. Chelsea joined in and posed with an alpaca. Then the girls decided they needed to take pictures with every animal in the Petting Zoo.

I got a great picture of a goat butting Eddie squarely in the butt. I instantly sent the photo to Paul and Manny, with the caption that said, "I just took a picture of a Butthead getting hit

44

in the butt!" They laughed hysterically. Eddie grabbed Paul's phone and saw the photo.

"Ha-ha, it's very funny until someone gets hurt," he said, as the goat nibbled at Eddie's vest making a small hole in one of the many pockets. Eddie pushed the goat away and continued lecturing. "Just because an animal is small doesn't mean it can't do damage." The persistent goat nibbled at the pocket again and was rewarded with a mini powdered sugar donut.

"Check out the goat, it has powdered sugar all over its face!" Manny laughed.

Everyone gathered around the goat to take photos. Eddie sighed, "That was my mid-morning snack…"

The next stop was the Aviary. It had a cool set of doors. The first door led into a small alcove or hallway. After the first door shut, the next door across from it opened. They never opened at the same time. I could tell that's how they kept the birds from escaping, by keeping them trapped in the alcove until they could shoo them back inside.

The Aviary was even bigger up close! It was so tall that the birds could fly around inside. They fluttered all over, and an ostrich came right up to me.

"Don't move, Josh," Eddie whispered from a safe distance away, "I've heard they'll peck you right in the eye."

I was terrified. I liked my brown eyes! I didn't want to lose them. I made myself get super still like a statue. I thought if I was still enough it would just go away. It seemed like I stood there forever. I felt beads of sweat running down my face.

"Eddie, help me," I whispered.

"Just stay calm, Josh. Don't talk. I'm gonna get a quarter and buy some bird food from that dispenser over there. Then I'll throw the food in the opposite direction to lure the ostrich away."

"Don't leave me…" I pleaded between clinched lips. I was pretty sure I had said it really clear, just like a ventriloquist.

I looked around for any other friends who could help me. From the corner of my eye, I saw them all further along the path. How could I signal to them that I needed help?

I saw Chelsea walk towards me. How could I signal for her to save herself? She was the one girl I really liked, and she had beautiful, big, brown eyes. What if the ostrich tried to peck them out? Too late, she was here and Eddie was still fumbling to get a quarter out of his backpack.

"Hi Josh," she said. "Why are you standing so still?"

"Say yorsell," I said between clinched lips.

"What?"

"Un…," I said telling her to run since she didn't get the hint when I said "save yourself."

"Gosh, what a cool looking bird," she said as she scratched the ostrich's head. It actually snuggled up to her for a second as if to say thank you and then trotted away.

"Now, what were you saying?" she asked.

"Oh, Eddie bet me I couldn't stand perfectly still for one minute without moving," I said and turned beet red hoping she wouldn't figure out how scared I just was.

"You two and your bets. You're so funny. Come on, let's catch up with the others," she said and we did just that.

After the Aviary, we came upon a sign that said "This way to the Lion's Den in Big Cat Country."

"I don't know if I really want to see a lion," Bria said quietly.

"I'm sure they caged them up really good," Manny told her.

"Really well," Marina interjected.

"I think I could fight them off long enough to let you guys escape," Eddie said, removing his backpack and riffling through it.

What could he possibly have in there that would fight off a bunch of lions?

As we all rounded the corner, we stopped dead in our tracks. Marina started laughing first and we all joined in. The Lion's Den was nothing but a playground for little kids with some picnic tables and a small food hut with vending machines inside.

Big Cat Country consisted of a few lions, tigers, and other big cats sleeping peacefully in their cages. They didn't roar or anything. I swear Eddie looked disappointed as he slung his backpack over his shoulders.

Lunch consisted of ham and cheese sand-wiches, potato chips, bananas and juice boxes, your typical field trip food. There wasn't a lot of conversation as we were all thinking about our upcoming kayak trek around Monkey Island. Hog told us we had to pick a buddy to share a kayak; no one could be alone. Since there were seven of us, that meant one of us would have to share a kayak with Freiberger. No volunteers yet.

"Any good stories, Eddie?" Manny broke the silence.

"Well, as a matter of fact, I do have one. In preparing for this overnight trip, I watched a show about animals that go wild. There was this elephant…"

"That's enough, Edward!" Ms. Freiberger stopped him. "I have a story and it's called let's finish lunch quietly."

Freiberger was not much of a storyteller.

After lunch, we made our way to the dock to get our kayaks. Paul and Manny paired up and so did me and Eddie. Hog said he would let the girls sit three to a kayak since they were much smaller. He said he would go with Ms. Freiberger, who looked none too pleased to be participating in this particular outing.

We suited up in our life jackets. Eddie had to take his safari vest off to fit the life jacket on. He put it in the kayak along with his backpack. We all took a bunch of pictures of each other standing by the sleek kayaks. The kayaks looked like short, plastic canoes. You had to sit on the bottom. We all took pictures of this too, which we immediately sent to our friends and our parents. Suddenly, out of nowhere Freiberger, freaked out.

"That is enough of the phoning with the texting and the sending! You all are so busy taking pictures that you're missing important safety information from Mr. Hog!" she said.

I guess she was kinda right, because I didn't even notice Hog was talking.

"I want each one of you to send one final message that will tell your parents that they will be receiving no more messages from you until tomorrow morning," she said as her eyes narrowed to slits. "Then you will turn your phones off and put them into this waterproof bag I have here. I brought it especially for this reason. In my day, we didn't send messages every five minutes! We experienced life, and now you will get a taste of that, as well. This texting is a distraction!"

"But we aren't just texting, we are making videos, too. It's really very creative. I can even put music and captions to it," Eddie said.

"Enough!" she screamed.

We were all too scared to do anything but what she asked. We reluctantly sent our last messages and handed our phones over. She carefully sealed the waterproof bag and put it in the bottom of her kayak. I wanted to tell her there was a small, waterproof storage area with a sealed lid in the back of each kayak in case your kayak tipped over, but I was too frightened.

After Freiberger had drained all the fun out of the trip, we paired up and shoved off. It didn't take long for us to forget about our phones as we began circling Monkey Island. It was glorious! The entire island was completely surrounded by a river. The edges of the island were grassy and there were tall trees in the middle of the island. It looked wild and a little scary, but fun too.

"Monkey Island was designed to be viewed from a kayak," Hog boasted knowingly. "Yep, ole Monkey Island. The crown jewel of the zoo. There live our small furry friends," he said and looked like he was about to cry. He must really love monkeys. "We can get pretty close, but we cannot dock on the island. It's their home and we must respect it."

"How do you get their food to them?" Bria asked.

"There is an underground tunnel that leads from the tree house to the island."

"Like the Chunnel?" Marina asked.

"Um yeah, like that," Hog said but I could tell he didn't know that the Chunnel was an underwater tunnel which connected England and France. We learned about in our social studies class.

I smelled the patas monkeys before I saw them. They smelled musky, like wet dogs. As we came around the river, I saw him. He was standing on a downed log that jutted out over the water and he really did look like a military colonel with his disapproving scowl and impressive mustache.

"That my friends, is the Colonel. He's the head monkey around here." Hog said.

"No way! What a great name. Just like the 'C' stands for in Chortles' name. He must be Chortles' dad. We named him after his dad and didn't even know it!" I said to Eddie.

"Oh my gosh!" Eddie exclaimed. "Josh, hand me my backpack. I need my binoculars. I've met this monkey before and he's a tricky one."

"What are you talking about...," I said and trailed off. Eddie was right. We had both met this monkey before and it hadn't ended well. It was a few years ago on a field trip when we were in the third grade. It was before Monkey Island was built and the monkeys lived in the Primate Palace. Eddie threw a banana at this very monkey and the monkey threw it right back! But it hit me, not Eddie. I had always wondered if the monkey thought I'd thrown it. And then I got my answer.

The Colonel looked at me and only me. He cocked his head to the side as if remembering the banana that had hit him all those years ago. Then he did something that chilled my soul. He put his index and middle finger to his eyes and then he pointed those two fingers at me.

"Don't panic, Josh," Eddie whispered, "but that monkey just gave you the universal 'I'm watching you,' sign."

Eddie was right. That was exactly what he had done. Everyone was staring at me in disbelief.

"I've never seen him do that before. Maybe you should paddle a bit further away from the island," Hog said.

I didn't have to be told twice as Eddie and I put the length of the river between me and the Colonel. Just then, the Colonel let out a tremendous cry. Then everything fell apart, and in slow motion, too.

Somehow Freiberger lost complete control of her kayak and steered it smack into a low hanging beehive on the opposite shore. Then she did something you should never do in a kayak. She stood up!

"I'm allergic!" she cried frantically, swatting at the bees that were encircling her face.

The girls were so freaked out by watching Freiberger, that their kayak ran straight into hers. Mayhem ensued as Freiberger's kayak tipped over dumping her and Hog into the water along with the bag of cellphones.

"I'll save her!" Eddie screamed and started pulling items out of his enormous backpack.

First, he pulled out some fins and removed his shoes and put them on. Then he donned a snorkel and a mask. He did a belly dive into the water while knocking the paddles out of the boat. The kayak rocked back and forth as I gripped the sides for dear life.

"Go Eddie!" the girls yelled for encouragement.

Eddie swam like crazy to get to Freiberger's overturned kayak. I watched in horror as the current swept the cellphone bag to Monkey Island. The girls were screaming, Eddie was swimming, Frieberger was flailing, Hog was dog paddling, and the monkeys were hollering and jumping up and down.

"Help," Ms. Freiberger gasped.

"You're almost to the shore!" Eddie yelled in between strokes, "Just stand up!"

Eddie waded to her and pulled her to safety on shore. Hog splashed out of the water and shouted, "I'll be right back," and ran away.

Manny, Paul and the girls joined Eddie and Freiberger on shore. I tried using my hands as paddles, but made little headway.

"Save the cellphone bag," Eddie shouted as he propped Freiberger up against a rock. He really kept calm in a crisis. Who knew?

I knew I needed to paddle towards the island. I figured it would be easier to turn my body around in the kayak, then to turn the actual kayak around. It took longer than I thought. Every little movement sent the kayak rocking back and forth. Finally, I got turned around and was facing the island. Just then I saw something truly terrible: There stood the Colonel on that same log jutting out over the water and I swear he was smiling. In his grubby little monkey paw he held up his new prize: The cellphone bag.

The Colonel

CHAPTER 6

I finally made it back to shore without the cellphones. That was one monkey I did not want to take on. Eddie hollered for his backpack and I raced it to him.

Eddie frantically pulled item after item out of his overstuffed bag. He flung the items over his shoulders as he pulled them out. "It's in here somewhere," he mumbled to himself.

"What are you looking for?" Marina asked.

"Anti-histamine to help with the swelling. Allie made me pack it because Josh is allergic to fire ants," he said as he flung a coiled rope out of his bag that, oddly enough landed perfectly around Manny's neck.

"I know that it helps with bee stings too, because I watched a show called, *When Nature Strikes,* that was all about allergic reactions to insect bites and stings," he continued as he flung his pocket knife out of the bag. Somehow it opened up in mid-air and landed right in the middle of the letter 'O' on the wooden Monkey Island sign. Bull's-eye.

The stings must have been too much for poor Freiberger. Her face and arms became swollen. It must have made her delirious because she started singing a song about birds, bees, trees and soda water fountains. It was pretty funny, except the part where she was hurting.

"Ah-ha!' Eddie said as he pulled a small first aid kit out of his bag. "Now for some water to wash it down." The frantic flinging of objects from his backpack continued. A flashlight soared through the air and I caught it one handed. Not bad, I thought to myself.

"Use my water, Eddie," Bria said as she gently pushed the hair back from Freiberger's brow.

Eddie tried to get her to swallow the pills, but Freiberger wasn't cooperating. She just kept on singing, "Where the lemonade springs and the bluebird sings…"

"Dang it, I can't get her to stop singing her song long enough to swallow the pills," Eddie said frustrated.

"Let me try, I know this song. My grandpa used to sing it." We sang the next line in unison; "It's the Big Rock Candy Mountain." Just as she was singing the next part which was a long, 'Oh-oh-oh-oh,' I popped two pills in her mouth and doused her quickly with the full bottle of water. She stammered and spit a bit, but they went down.

"Genius!" Eddie exclaimed.

Just then, Hog arrived with a golf cart. We helped carry Freiberger to the cart so Hog could take her to the first aid station. He did not wait for us to climb aboard. He just took off at top speed.

"I guess we're walking back," Eddie said as he stuffed the scattered items back into his backpack.

We all helped him gather his things. Manny was still wearing the coiled rope around his neck where Eddie had unintentionally flung it. As he took it off and handed it to Eddie, he said, "It's a darn good thing you packed that medicine."

"Yep, you can never be too prepared. It's just like I was saying before about the *what-ifs*." Eddie said.

"Oh, I get it now," Paul said.

"Wait!" I yelled. Everyone turned my way. "What if Hog gives Freiberger even more medicine? Could it hurt her?"

We all looked at each other and took off running. As we fled, the Colonel watched us from across the water, handing out our cell phones as prizes to his troop.

I chewed on a piece of beef jerky that Eddie had produced from his seemingly bottomless backpack. It was spicy and greasy and delicious. We all sat around the lobby of the Tree House waiting to hear how Freiberger was doing. A plump woman with curly brown hair entered the room. She had introduced herself earlier as Ms. Velasquez and told us she was the nurse on duty at the zoo.

"Okay kids," she said, "Ms. Freiberger will be fine. Hog is in there with her right now. She is sleeping and will be out for the rest of the day and possibly into the night. She may get up every now and then, but she will be a bit loopy. Eddie, it was good of you to give her anti-histamine, I just wish I would have known that before I dosed her, too. She's out for the count, but she's safe. You kids better call your parents to come and get you."

"Oh, that's not necessary," I said. Nothing was going to spoil this night.

"I hardly think you kids should stay here without a teacher," she said.

"He means it's not be necessary because we already called our parents. They're on their way right now." Eddie said with an innocent look on his face.

"What about Ms. Freiberger?" she asked.

"My mom said we would drop her off at her sister's house," he answered without missing a beat. He really was the king of lying.

"Her sister, huh?" she said not wholly convinced.

"Yeah, her name is Ms. Sniedendorf. She's was married once, of course. That's why they have different last names."

The lie worked! It must have been the details that did the trick, 'cause Ms. Velasquez nodded. "Fine. I am going to leave. I need to get home to my family. I've stayed too long already," she said and left the building.

Just then Hog entered the lobby. "Did I miss anything?"

"Nope. Ms. Velasquez said our teacher will be fine and that you're in charge," Eddie said.

Hog swelled up with pride. You could tell that he was rarely left in charge. "Well, it's too late to continue our tour so let's lock up the zoo. Then it's off to the classroom for a tranquilizer gun demonstration," he said, jingling his keys.

We all high-fived and fist-bumped Eddie for saving our field trip.

A little while later, after Eddie changed into some dry clothes, we met downstairs. We all squished into the golf cart to make our rounds to lock up the zoo. Hog, Paul and Manny sat up front, the three girls squished in the back, and Eddie and I stood on the back floorboard and hung onto either side. It was a blast. I felt like I owned the zoo.

I looked over at Eddie. He was grinning from ear to ear. He looked like a young but slightly chubby safari hunter, with his many pocketed vest and cool khaki pants. *You know, Eddie was right, a safari hat and matching canteen would complete his look.*

Hog checked all the cages and made sure the animals had food and water. Then he locked the big bamboo entrance doors when the last guest left. The zoo was finally ours! I couldn't wait to explore it. What freedom! A whole zoo full of wild animals, safely in cages of course, and no teachers to pester us. Just Hog to boss us around and heck, he was kind of a big kid himself.

I enjoyed the feeling of wind on my face as we rode back to the Tree House. It felt warm and strong and I smiled to myself. But then, a few moments later, the wind changed quickly from warm to cool.

"Did you feel that, Josh?" Eddie asked as the wind gusted warm again.

"Yep," I said, and felt a pit in my stomach as the ever-changing wind went back and forth by several degrees, blowing first warm from the east and then cool from the west.

"A storm's a-brewing," Hog said just as a large clap of thunder rang out across the sky.

"A storm's a brewing?" I said under my breath to Eddie. "Who says that?"

"A sailor?" Eddie answered and dug in the side pocket of his backpack and produced a little bundle of material shaped like a cylinder. After undoing a couple of snaps, he opened up what became an umbrella which he held over his head as fat raindrops began to bombard us all. The top of the golf cart protected everyone else, so really I was the only one getting wet.

We entered the Tree House and followed Hog to one of the classrooms upstairs. Eddie tossed me a chamois cloth he produced from his backpack.

"What's this?" I asked.

"It's a chamois cloth," he said pronouncing it 'shammy cloth.' "It's able to soak up huge amounts of water at once."

Come to think of it, I remembered my dad using one like it to dry the car after he washed it. I smelled it. Phew! It smelled oily, like an old car. "Was this Dad's?"

"Yeah, he threw it out. Can you believe it? It's still perfectly good."

I used the chamois cloth to dry my arms, legs, hair and face. It felt a little greasy, but it got the job done."

"Hey everyone," I said, "Look how much water I soaked up," and I squeezed the water in a nearby sink for effect. Everyone busted a gut.

"All right, calm down now. It's time to get started," Hog said. "I have something special for all of you."

He reached into a bag and produced seven, Junior Zookeeper Badges. They were shaped like police badges and were gold and shiny. The words, "*Junior Zookeeper*" were imprinted on the badge. "By accepting these badges, you have entered into a sacred pact and pledge to uphold the safety and the security of our City Zoo."

We eagerly accepted the badges. Then Hog reached into a desk drawer and pulled out a gun.

"We get guns, too!" Eddie exclaimed.

"Hang on, fella," Hog said. "This is a tranquilizer gun, for grown-ups only."

Oohs and ahhs from my classmates.

"We use them to subdue animals when we need to give them a medical checkup. I don't need to tell you, some of the animals can be pretty dangerous."

"How does it work?" Paul asked.

"Well, you see, you get a tranquilizer dart," he said and pulled a tranquilizer dart out of the desk drawer. "And then you put a tranquilizer dart in this slot," he said as he loaded the gun. "This is enough to take down a 200 pound animal, which, oddly enough, is what I weigh. Next, we load the drowsy animal onto a stretcher." Hog pointed to a long row of different sized stretchers lined up against the wall. "Then we carry the animal to the medical facility located directly behind the old Primate Palace."

"When you shoot the animal, does it hurt?" Marina asked.

"Let me demonstrate. I'll need a few actors to help set the scene: Chubs and Mustache, how 'bout you two? You can be the animals," he said to me and Eddie as he waved the gun around carelessly.

Usually when someone calls Eddie chubby, it does not end well. This time, however, he was laughing really hard.

"What's so funny?" I asked.

"I dunno, Mustache. What is so funny?" Eddie giggled.

Chelsea produced a small mirror from her bag and held it up for me to see. Some leftover oil from the chamois cloth was on my face, under my nose to be precise. It looked just like a greasy caterpillar. I wiped it off with my sleeve.

"Not cool, Eddie," I muttered under my breath. "Or should I say 'Chubs.'"

Then Eddie got a look in his eye. A look I hadn't seen for a very long while. It was the look of a former bully who just got pushed a little too far. "Take it back, Josh. Now." He said through clenched teeth.

I felt a little bad about calling him Chubs. Eddie had lost a huge amount of weight since last year when he was the bully of our elementary school. I'm sure from an outsider's point of view he still looked a little chubby, but to those of us who knew him, he was just a big guy who didn't bully us anymore. Still, it did not give him the right to do what he did to me.

"You gave me that chamois just to embarrass me." I was convinced it was some kind of secret plot to make me look stupid in front of Chelsea.

"Now here is a great example of two angry animals getting ready to 'throw down' as we say in the zoo field," Hog said. "If I were in the wild, I would point the gun at the biggest animal." He nodded to Eddie. "Then reload quickly and go for the scrawny one last." He nodded to me.

Eddie and I turned our heads and stared at Hog. He carelessly aimed the gun at us as if it wasn't loaded with enough tranquilizer serum to take us both down.

"Whoa, mister, put that down," Eddie said.

"You're going to hurt someone," I added.

"What? Now don't get all worried. I have done this a thousand times," he said.

"Really?" I asked.

"Well, no. But I've seen it done a thousand times. It's easy, really. Like I said, you just get in your shooter stance and then point and shoot. Like this." Hog pointed the gun at a poster of a gorilla. As he was getting in his shooter stance, he tripped over an electrical cord and stumbled. We all heard the gun go

THWAK as it released the tranquilizer. From that point on, everything happened in slow motion.

I threw myself to the ground. I saw Hog hit the desk, knocking it over and sending the contents flying. A bunch of sharpened pencils flew through the air and rained down from above like Robin Hood's arrows. They were all headed straight for Manny. I saw him bob and weave deftly, never letting one make contact as they continued to fall around him.

A stapler tumbled end over end in the air and made a beeline for Paul. It opened in mid-flight like a mechanical shark swimming in for its kill. Eddie tackled Paul to the ground just in the nick of time as the stapler missed them both by inches.

A storm of paperclips pelted the girls as they took shelter under a desk.

Someone yelled loudly, "Man Down!" But I wasn't sure who.

As I surveyed the scene, it looked like a bomb had gone off. Table and chairs were overturned, office supplies littered the floor, and clothes were torn. I noticed all my friends standing up, kind of shell shocked. Then I saw Hog. He stumbled all around the room, shouting, "Man Down!" He looked like a big, clumsy zombie.

"Who's down?" I asked. I looked around, and all my friends seemed fine, although a little out of sorts.

"Man Dooooooooown...." Hog trailed off and fell face down on the floor. That's when I noticed the tranquilizer dart sticking out of his butt cheek.

"How did it get there?" I asked.

We all looked at the gorilla poster. It had a tiny hole in it. Then we looked back at Hog's butt. *Did it ricochet? How?*

"What a shot!" Eddie exclaimed.

CHAPTER 7

It took all seven of us to load Hog onto the stretcher to take him to the first aid station. We barely fit in the elevator, but we were afraid we'd drop him if we tried the stairs. After we plopped him onto the cot next to Freiberger, we covered him with a blanket and tucked him in. Freiberger was snoring loudly, so I guess she was fine.

"This is bad. We should probably call our parents," Marina said.

"What? Are you crazy? We have the entire zoo to ourselves. That never happens. Let's take advantage of the situation," Eddie said.

"I agree...," I said.

"Thanks, Josh," Eddie said.

"No, I agree with Marina. We need to call our parents," I added.

"Maybe we should vote on it? Who wants to stay? I mean it is our duty as Junior Zookeepers to make sure that the zoo is safe and secure. Plus, the rain has let up a little. Raise your hands if you're with me," Eddie argued persuasively.

Manny and Paul raised their hands. When I saw Chelsea raise her hand, I raised mine, too.

"Josh!" Marina wailed.

"I just got to thinking that maybe Eddie's right," I said. "I mean, really what else could go wrong..." *I wasn't ready to give up spending time with Chelsea now that I thought about it.*

"Well, then Bria and I are going to call our parents," Marina said, although Bria didn't look as sure as before.

"Alright. Since you two are going to blow it for us anyway, how 'bout a farewell dinner before we go home? Hog said there was grub in the Canopy Café. I'm sure he wouldn't care if we made a couple of sandwiches." Eddie smiled innocently.

"I am a little hungry," Bria said quietly.

"Fine! Then let's eat and get out of here." Marina huffed.

"Eddie! Eddie! Eddie!" my friends all chanted as Eddie attempted to make the world's biggest sandwich.

"Calm down, calm down. This is just the first layer," Eddie said.

Eddie decided he was going to make a sandwich using every lunch meat known to man.

"Alright, the bologna layer is finished. Josh, what else is there?" Eddie said.

I went back into the walk-in cooler to see what else I could find. The walk-in cooler was huge. Really huge, and very cold. It felt like stepping into a fridge. It was about the size of a small room and was filled from floor to ceiling with food stacked on shelves. I felt like it should have been called the "fridgeroom."

I stumbled out a few moments later loaded down with meats and cheeses.

"A little help here!" I yelled as my friends came to relieve me of my groceries.

Eddie had found the world's longest loaf of bread. It was a crusty French loaf that was a good three or four feet long.

"This may get messy," Eddie said as he reached into the front pocket of his safari vest and pulled out a pair of plastic safety goggles. Thunder boomed as the storm began to pick up again. I noticed a crazed look in Eddie's eyes.

"This will be my greatest creation ever!" He laughed like a mad scientist and started piling meat and cheese on top of the bologna at an incredible speed. What a drama king.

He used all the lunchmeat and cheese I'd brought out of the cooler except one. All that remained in a lone zip-locked bag was a meat labeled HEADCHEESE.

Eddie and I looked at each other and yelled "Sniedendorf!" as lightening flashed outside.

"Where?" Manny said looking around nervously.

"Nowhere, Manny." I started laughing with Eddie. "Sniedendorf likes headcheese," I held up the bag so everyone could see. This made everyone say, "Ew!"

Sniedendorf was the scariest and meanest substitute teacher we ever had in elementary school. Freiberger really was her sister, or so the rumors go. Sniedendorf was legendary for eating headcheese sandwiches! Last year when I was forced to eat lunch next to her, I overheard her say headcheese was made from the brains of a pig. Eddie was convinced it was zombie food.

"Hurry up, Eddie. It looks like the storm is getting worse and we haven't called home," Marina said.

"You can't rush a masterpiece," Eddie said, running his fingers through his hair. It stuck up at crazy angles making him look even more like a mad scientist, especially with the goggles still on.

"Okay, time for condiments," Eddie said.

I noticed the girls getting nervous because the rain was pelting the windows really hard. "Maybe if we all help, we'll get done faster," I said as I grabbed a squeeze bottle of mustard.

Everyone started grabbing condiments to pile on the massive sandwich as the lights began flickering.

"Hurry! Hurry!" I heard myself yelling.

Eddie gently placed the top of the loaf on the enormous sandwich. He reached into yet another pocket of his vest and pulled out a tape measure. He started to measure the sandwich's height, "And now…the finale! Supper-time!"

Just then a CRACK of lightning blinded us temporarily while a BOOM of thunder shook the tree house. Then everything went pitch black.

From the total darkness I heard Eddie say, "Now would be a good time to call our parents."

CHAPTER 8

I stood in the darkness for what seemed like several minutes. Not breathing, just listening. When did the storm get so bad? Just then I saw the biggest lightening flash of my entire life. With its quick burst of light I caught a glimpse of all my friends. I saw Chelsea, Bria and Paul huddled under the table, Manny and Marina clung to each other for dear life and Eddie was chomping down on a slice of the sandwich he'd made.

"Calm down," Eddie said with his mouth full. "It's going to be alright. I've got a flashlight right here," he said and produced a keychain flashlight out of his vest pocket.

He turned it on. Blue streaks of light shone around the Café making everything look eerie. "Follow me downstairs and we can call our parents," he said, as he handed out slices of his big sandwich. Surprisingly, I was hungry.

Eddie led the way down the stairs with his flashlight shining the way. We walked behind him in a single line, holding on to one another with one hand and holding onto our sandwiches with the other hand. The only sounds were sneakers on the stairs and the occasional swallow. It was a good sandwich!

When we got to the lobby, Marina picked up the phone on the information desk. "No dial tone! And our cell phones are on Monkey Island!" she wailed.

"That big crack we heard must have been a tree falling. It probably took out the phone lines," Paul added.

"Just great! Thanks a lot, Eddie. Now we're really stuck here." Marina huffed.

"Then it's our job as Junior Zookeepers to make sure the zoo is safe and secure," Eddie said.

"I'm not going out in this storm!" Marina said, and we all murmured in agreement.

"It will be over soon, I'm sure. We need to check to make sure all the animals are safe. Who's with me?"

No one answered Eddie.

"Okay, okay. I get it; we aren't as prepared as we should be. Wait! The gift shop!" Eddie threw his light in the direction of the gift shop. "Follow me!" he yelled enthusiastically.

We huddled together and followed Eddie. Eddie tried to open up the gift shop but could not. "Dang, it's locked. Hold on. Hog must have the keys. You guys wait right here, I'll be right back." Eddie ran towards the first aid station then stopped and turned back. "Hey, maybe you should come with me, Josh."

I knew it. When I'm with Eddie, I always end up on the wrong side of right. "Fine, but let's make it quick," I said.

We entered the first aid station and it was as if there was a snoring competition going on. I couldn't tell which one was louder, Hog or Freiberger. "Just hurry," I said to Eddie.

"Don't you think I know that? There could be animals running loose and causing mischief all over the place," Eddie said.

"No, I meant let's hurry so we can get back to our friends. Do you really think there are animals running loose?"

"Well, if you were a caged animal wouldn't you want to escape and play with all the other animals?" Eddie asked.

"I dunno, maybe."

Eddie gently rolled Hog over and retrieved the keys from his belt loop. He didn't wake up and he didn't stop snoring either.

"Got 'em! Let's go," he said.

I followed Eddie back to our gang.

"There sure are a lot of keys on this key ring." Eddie tried key after key but none of them worked. He had one key left. "Hope this is it!"

BINGO! It worked! Eddie made a beeline straight for the safari hats with the cool lights on them. We followed him eagerly.

"Here," he handed one to each of us. "Put them on and turn on the lights." We did. The room lit up like the 4th of July. You could hear a collective sigh of relief.

Normally, I'm not afraid of the dark but it was much, much better with lots of light.

"Isn't this stealing?" Marina asked.

"Not if we return them when we are done. It's just borrowing," Eddie said.

Marina didn't look convinced.

"So, now what?" Paul asked.

Eddie inspected our hats and announced, "Getting prepared was the first step. The second step is to go back up to Canopy Café."

"Why? Are you still hungry?" I asked.

"What? No, Josh. We need to get a look around the zoo and the best view is from up there. But now that you mention it, I did see some potato chips." Eddie raised his fist for a fistbump, but I ignored him. He put his fist down.

Marina asked, "What makes you think you can see anything in the dark? All the lights in the zoo are out."

Eddie pulled a pair of binoculars out of his backpack. "My secret weapon," he said.

No reaction from any of us.

"What's the difference between your binoculars and those up there? It's still too dark to see outside," Manny asked.

I already knew the answer to Manny's question. These particular binoculars were a sore subject in our house. Eddie had saved up all his Christmas, birthday and chore money just to buy them.

"They're night vision binoculars!" Eddie boasted.

When Eddie first got them, he would sit in the dark and wait for me to enter our bedroom, and then he would scare me. He even scared our mom and dad, but he never scared our baby sister. Needless to say, Eddie was banned from using the binoculars inside the house. So now he uses them outside, to look for animals and such. Sometimes he watches for the Swamp Ape, but hasn't seen it yet.

"Okay, let's go back upstairs," Eddie said. "I'll tell you a story on the way. It's a tale of

Treefoot, a distant, but smaller cousin of the Swamp Ape."

Oh no, not again. Even in a crisis, Eddie was still the master storyteller. As we climbed the stairs, the story unfolded.

"Of course, you all already know about the Swamp Ape, a hairy Bigfoot type that lives deep in the swampy marshes of the Florida Everglades. But I bet you don't know about Treefoot or how it got its name," Eddie said as we continued up the stairs.

"Wow! I wonder why we didn't learn about them in school?" Paul said.

"Excuse me? Are you hearing yourselves? We have never learned about them in school because neither one of those animals exists," Marina said.

"How do you know? Is it because you have never seen one? You know, I have never seen oxygen, but I know it exists," Eddie answered.

"Of course oxygen exists. That has already been proven," Marina said.

"But you do agree that you can't see oxygen, right?"

"Right."

"My point exactly. You can't see oxygen, but it's there. Just like the Swamp Ape. Everybody knows they are masters of camouflage, so it's hard to spot them in the wild. Their shaggy fur blends in perfectly with tree bark and swamp moss. The only thing that tips you off that one is nearby is the smell. They smell like twenty wet dogs mixed in with one wet cat." He smiled triumphantly.

"I think Eddie's right. Only a few people have seen them, like my cousin's best friend's brother. He saw the Swamp Ape crossing the road when he was driving home really late one night," Manny said.

"Is this the same guy whose head blew off from eating pop rocks and drinking soda at the same time?" Marina asked.

"Yes."

"Manny, how could he see the Swamp Ape if his head blew off from mixing pop rocks and soda?"

"I guess it happened before his head blew off."

"Well, then that does make perfect sense," Marina said sarcastically.

"I'm so glad you believe now," Eddie said oblivious to Marina's sarcasm.

We finally reached the top of the stairs and entered the Canopy Café. Our helmet flashlights created a cool strobe light effect as we looked around the restaurant.

"You never finished your story about the Treefoot," Paul said to Eddie.

Eddie held his hand up to Paul like one soldier does to another to warn them to be silent.

"No time for that now," Eddie whispered as he scanned the room from left to right with his night vision goggles. "We have a mission at hand."

Eddie tip-toed across the room like a ninja. We all watched silently. *Did he see something we didn't see?* He veered toward the kitchen. We all stayed where we were.

Once Eddie was in the kitchen, we could no longer see him. However, we could hear a faint rustling noise.

"You okay, Eddie?" I barely managed to get out.

No answer. The rustling noise was getting louder. It sounded like he was struggling with something or someone.

"Maybe we should go help him," Manny said.

"Um, yeah, maybe," Paul responded.

Then the rustling noise got so loud that we all jumped back about two feet.

"Got it!" Eddie yelled.

What did he get? Was it an animal?

Eddie walked over with something behind his back. Chelsea grab Bria's hand. I couldn't blame her. I was nervous too.

Eddie whipped his hands high above our heads, "Barbeque or Original?" he said.

We all looked up. He was holding two very large bags of potato chips.

"That's what all that noise was? You, looking for chips?" Manny asked.

"Um, yeah. Why?" Eddie said.

"It sounded like you were fighting with an animal in there." Marina sounded mad.

"No, I was just grabbing some chips. But then I saw some barbeque ones way at the top of the pantry. I had to climb up to get them, and it was kinda a struggle. Hey, wait! You guys thought I was fighting with an animal and no one came to help me?" Eddie said.

"We thought about it," Paul said shamefully.

Eddie looked at me.

I felt guilty. "Okay, new rule: No matter what happens, we always help each other out. Animals or no animals, scared or not scared. Agreed?" I asked everyone.

Eddie put his hand in first and I put mine on top of his, then Paul, Manny, Bria, Chelsea and finally Marina. "Agreed," we all said.

CHAPTER 9

We were sitting in a circle listening to Eddie. I was munching away on the barbeque chips. They were tasty. I was glad Eddie went the extra mile to get them.

"See, the Treefoot apes were mad because they were so much smaller than their Swamp Ape cousins. They didn't think that was fair at all. They were especially jealous of the Swamp Apes' giant feet," Eddie explained.

"Why?, What's the big deal?" Manny asked. He was rather short himself.

"That's just it, it's not a big deal. But in the swamp world, size matters. So they had find a way to make their feet bigger."

"What did they do?" I asked. Eddie had lured me in again. And not just me, we were all inching closer to Eddie as he continued.

"It was really hard, but they knew they had to do it." He paused to wolf down a handful of chips. We waited.

"They took the oldest Treefoot first. They made him stand on top of a tree stump and then they all took turns pulling on his feet. Really hard. They were trying to stretch them out. At first, they didn't see any changes, so they got some vines and tree branches and wrapped his feet in those. It was easier to pull his feet when they were wrapped with the branches. Within a short time, they noticed his feet getting bigger and longer. Then they all repeated the process, down to the tiniest Treefoot. However, they soon got tired. Don't forget they were smaller than the Swamp Ape and therefore much weaker."

"So, did they stop?" Chelsea asked.

"Yes, that is exactly what they did. They fell asleep. Some say for twenty years, other say a hundred years. I think it was closer to fifty years, judging by what happened."

"What happened?" Manny asked.

"If you guys keep interrupting him, we will never hear the end," Marina said.

"Thanks, Marina," Eddie said.

"I'm not trying to help you, Eddie. I want you to finish your story, so we can figure out what to do about this situation we are in." She huffed.

"Oh well, then let me wrap it up." He cleared his throat. "As I was saying, they woke up to horrible screams. But because they were Treefoot, their screams sounded like songs with made up words like HOOS and WAHS!"

"That's awful. Why were they screaming?" Bria asked.

"Because something very weird happened to them: When the oldest one finally woke up, he noticed that his feet were not only big and long, but they had also turned into actual tree roots, with branches sprouting out. He looked around at all the other Treefoot and saw that their feet were the same! It had happened during their sleep. His screams woke the others and then they all screamed when they saw their feet. The littlest Treefoot was so scared that he ran behind a tree to get away from himself. That's when they realized the coolest thing."

"What?" Paul asked.

"Camouflage."

"Huh?" I asked.

"They couldn't see the tiniest Treefoot because his new tree legs blended in with the tree he was standing behind."

Oohs and aahs from all of us.

"And so, that's how they got their name. You can tell when they're close because of their song-screams. But you can't see them of course, because they look just like trees."

With that Eddie turned off his helmet light and said, "The end."

The room dimmed a little without his light on, but we didn't care. We all clapped enthusiastically. He sure was a good storyteller.

Then, I heard a sound that chilled my soul. My head shot in the direction of the window on my right. I just heard a WAH!

Lightning flashed. I saw two small eyes peer through the enormous Canopy Café window. It was a Treefoot!

"T...T...T...Treefoot!" I stammered and pointed to the window.

"Very funny, Josh," Eddie said.

"No, I saw it. I swear! It was right outside the window. Didn't you hear the WAH?"

"Knock it off, you're scaring the girls."

"I'm not scared," Marina said.

"I am," Manny whispered.

"Wait for the next lightning flash. You'll see," I pleaded.

"Fine, but if we're going to waste valuable time then we should relax and refuel," Eddie said.

He arranged some chairs in a semi-circle facing the window where I'd just seen the Treefoot. We all sat down like we were at a movie theater getting ready to watch a feature film. Eddie passed the bag of chips around and everyone began to munch happily, except me. I was too nervous. My stomach was doing flip-flops.

It didn't take very long for lightning to strike again. You could see every tree as clear as day, but no Treefoot was anywhere to be found.

"I think we're safe from the big, bad Treefoot," Marina scoffed.

Just then we all heard a loud HOOO!

"See! That's it!" I declared triumphantly.

"Oh, no! Josh is right! He's coming to get us!" Manny yelled and hid under a nearby table. Bria and Chelsea decided to join him.

"Calm down. That was probably just an owl," Marina said.

I ran to the window and pointed outside. I felt like I was going crazy. "I swear it was out there," I said.

I turned around to face my friends with my back to the window. Another loud lightning cracked and I was blinded for a second. When my eyes refocused, I noticed all my friends looked like they had seen a ghost.

"Don't turn around, Josh," Eddie said, his eyes as big as saucers. "Just walk away from the window, slowly."

To this day, I'll never understand why I turned around. But when I did, I was face-to-face with it! It was scruffy looking, with a mustache, and had a mouth full of razor sharp teeth. The only thing between us was a pane of glass and I'm guessing not the thickest of glass either. The creature let out a fearsome battle cry; HOOO! I answered with a throaty scream of AHHHH! We continued screaming for what seemed like days, locked in some bizarre duel of sound. Finally, it gave a final grunt and swung away to the nearest tree.

I turned around exhausted and a little battle weary. "I did it," I gasped. "I out screamed the Treefoot and scared him off. You're welcome."

"Ah, Josh, that was no Treefoot. It was the Colonel," Eddie said.

My furry nemesis!

"But how?" was all I could say.

Eddie was already at the window with his night vision binoculars. "Looks like a tree is down on Monkey Island. It made a bridge over the water to the zoo side. I can see the rest of the monkeys escaping. The Colonel must have been the first one to cross over the tree trunk and the others must have decided to follow him."

"Well, this is just great. Now we have wild monkeys running all over the zoo." Marina said. "We need to wake up Hog."

"He's not going to wake up," I said. "He's really out."

"Alright, this is not a drill people," Eddie said in a very commanding voice. "We've got a serious situation here. As newly appointed Junior Zookeepers, it is our job to save the monkeys."

"No, it isn't! It's just a fake badge, Eddie. We are not real Junior Zookeepers." Marina said.

"I don't know about the rest of you guys, but I took a pledge and I mean to honor it."

"But what about the storm? We could get struck by lightning," she said.

"Yeah, Eddie. We'd better wait until the storm blows over before heading outside. Just to be safe," I said, knowing the storm could rage on for hours at this rate. At least I hoped it would. I didn't want to get any closer to the Colonel than I already had.

Eddie looked like he was thinking real hard. I could tell he was struggling with his duty to save the monkeys over his fear of becoming a human lightning rod.

"Marina's right. We shouldn't go out into the storm. We could get hurt. And as your leader and captain, I am responsible for the team," Eddie said. "But as soon as the rain stops, it's all hands on deck."

"Thanks Eddie, but I don't remember anyone putting you in charge," Marina said.

A chorus of "Yeahs" sounded from the group plus one "I'm good with that," from Manny.

"I'm a fair guy. Let's vote then," he said. "Who else wants to be the team captain?"

"Me," Paul said.

"Me too," Marina added.

"And me," I said. I didn't really want to be captain; I just wanted to prolong the conversation so we could stay inside.

"I think the best way to proceed is to have a debate. You know, we could make a speech and take questions from the audience about our qualifications to be captain," Marina said.

"What audience? We're not running for president," I said. Eddie and Marina were on some weird power trip.

"I'm out," Paul muttered. Everyone knew he hated making speeches.

"Me too," I said. So much for my input.

"I think it's an excellent idea," Eddie said. "Let's take five minutes to think of what we want to say and meet right back here for the debate."

Eddie and Marina went to different corners of the room. Eddie took the barbeque chips with him because he said he thought better while eating. I stayed with Manny, Paul, and the girls. I hoped that I was the only one to notice that the storm was slowly abating. It was just slightly drizzling now. The thunder-claps were far in the distance.

When the five minutes were up, the storm had abated. No more lighting or thunder, and not even a single raindrop was falling. Great, now whatever our plans were, they could no longer be postponed by weather. I secretly hoped that everyone chose Eddie. He seemed to really shine in crisis situations.

"Are you ready, Eddie?" Marina asked.

"Yep, ladies first," he said.

Marina stood in front of us. Our helmet lights shone on her. "Okay, first this field trip has been doomed from the beginning. I don't see any way to salvage it."

Paul raised his hand. Marina looked at him, "Yes?"

"What does salvage mean?" Paul asked.

"It means to fix or make it better," Marina continued. "So, what I suggest is we come up with a plan to get in touch with our parents and get out of here."

"How do we do that?" Eddie asked

"Well, I'm not sure yet."

"You did have five minutes," Eddie said.

"Yes, but I was focusing more on a general plan, not specifics." Marina sighed.

"You would never make it in the special forces," Eddie quipped.

"Aw, Eddie, cut her some slack," Paul said.

"Fine, I thought we were supposed to ask questions," Eddie said.

"Yes, but that wasn't a question," Chelsea added. "It was just mean."

"I'm sorry, Marina. Please continue," Eddie backed off.

"We could double check each room to see if there is a cell phone somewhere or a radio. If that doesn't work, we could head to our rooms and wait out the night for the workers to get here early and have them get in touch with our parents. Thank you very much." She gave a little bow.

Bria and Chelsea clapped.

Really? That was it. I had higher hopes for Marina. Maybe it was a little scarier for the girls to be stuck here. Wait, that can't be. Any one of these girls could kick my butt at any given time. Maybe they just wanted to go home.

Eddie cleared his throat and began. "Well, I for one do believe that this field trip can be *salvaged*." He used a finger quote gesture in the air when he said salvaged. I guarantee he just learned that word, but boy he used it well.

"The way I see it, we only have one option. As Junior Zookeepers, it is our responsibility to keep this zoo safe. We can't have monkeys running around all night. Who knows what kind of destruction they could cause. What if they let the lions out? They are smart, but we are smarter. We have to get them back onto Monkey Island, and we need to do this before morning, and I know just how to do it! Who's with me?"

Silence filled the room. Was Eddie serious? Capture monkeys, was that even possible?

"Come on, you guys. When have you ever been in a situation where you got to be the heros? We could have an amazing adventure together. I could probably do this by myself, but it would work better if we band together as a team. It would be the greatest story ever, legendary I dare say."

I raised my hand. "Do you have a plan?"

"Yes. I took my five minutes seriously. Wanna hear it?"

Not only was everyone nodding their heads yes, but we all seemed to inch closer to Eddie, even Marina. Sometimes Eddie was like the Pied Piper.

Treefoot, smaller cousin of the Swamp Ape.

CHAPTER 10

We were in the lobby of the Tree House, huddled together playing with our new Special Operations equipment. We'd gathered walkie-talkies from the administrative offices. We felt like real Junior Zookeepers. It was exciting.

"Okay, looks like we are ready. We'll head to Monkey Island first. We need to do some recon work there," Eddie said.

"What is recon?" Bria asked.

"Are you making up words now?" Marina huffed.

"No. I was watching this cool show on the military channel and they used that word a lot. It stands for recognizant and means to gather information about the enemy, their where-abouts and plans, stuff like that."

"The monkeys aren't our enemies," Marina added.

"Speak for yourself," I mumbled.

"Josh is right, they are targeting him. The Colonel doesn't like him at all," Eddie said. "Who knows what they have planned for him. It could be a luau with Josh as the guest of honor, if you know what I mean."

"Whaaat? You think they want to eat me?"

"I think we might be getting a little crazy here. They are not after Josh and monkeys don't eat people," Marina said frustrated.

"I don't know, one night I was watching this show on *National Geographic* and these monkeys were really hungry and…" Eddie stopped when he noticed Chelsea was crying.

I didn't realize how upset she was. I didn't like seeing her cry. "Chelsea, don't worry. Nobody's going to get eaten. We're just going to help get the monkeys back on their island."

"Maybe the girls should stay here while we go out," Manny offered.

Chelsea stopped crying. "No way. We all said we would do this together. I'm fine now. I just don't like the thought of Josh getting eaten."

I didn't either. Nice to know at least one of my friends didn't want me to become monkey food.

"Okay, troops. Let's move out." Eddie led us outside.

It didn't take us long to get to Monkey Island. The storm had blown over and a huge full moon provided much needed light. We saw how the monkeys had escaped. The tree that fell over during the storm had left a perfect bridge over the water. We all just stared at it. It was pretty big, definitely big enough for us to cross over.

"Well, I guess we better cross and see if there are any monkeys left on the island," Eddie suggested.

"Who's first?" Paul asked.

"It should be boy, girl, boy, girl, boy, girl, boy. I will go first, Josh you go last," Eddie ordered.

Of course, I would be last. The story of my life.

The bark of the tree felt slippery and rough at the same time. I was on all fours like a dog, as I crossed the downed tree. I saw the swirling torrent of water below me. I was sweating even though it wasn't hot outside. I wasn't sure why I was afraid. I was actually a pretty good swimmer and knew I'd be okay if I slipped off. I think I was more worried about a surprise attack from the Colonel. I was the last person to cross, but the first person in the line of fire.

"Stop clowning around, Josh!" Eddie called safely from the other side.

He'd just walked across it like it was regular bridge. Come to think of it, so did everyone else.

I bravely stood up to save face. I kept my arms out to help me balance. I was at the halfway point when I heard a tremendous SQUAWK! It was followed by several more squawks that were coming from the front of the zoo.

"The monkeys are in the Aviary!" Eddie yelled. "Follow me, team!"

Eddie started back the way he came, but at full speed. This guy was afraid of nothing! I saw his big frame barreling toward me with all my friends in tow. It was kind of intimidating so I dropped back down to all fours again. I was scrambling as fast as I could, but it wasn't fast enough. Eddie was getting ready to slam full force into me. I could see from his expression, he couldn't stop in time. Suddenly, everything went into slow motion.

"Noooooo!" Eddie said. He was about to impact me full on. I could see the whites of his eyes and somehow I could see the fear on my friends faces behind him, too. They were all too close. If Eddie and I went down, it would be a pile up for everyone.

And then I did something I didn't even know I could do. I dropped on my belly and hugged the tree trunk with my arms and my legs. Somehow, I twisted myself under the tree trunk. My arms and legs held true as my body swayed under the tree just feet from the churning water.

Eddie's big cave man feet hit the trunk perfectly between my feet and my hands, just where my back had been a few seconds ago. Followed by more feet in order of girl, boy, girl, boy and girl. When the last pair passed me, I scrambled back up and casually walked the rest of the way. All my friends cheered.

"That was so cool!" Eddie exclaimed.

"Yeah, you were like some kind of acrobat," Manny added.

It was kind of cool, I thought to myself.

"I didn't know you were so strong and flexible," Chelsea added.

I practically swooned until Paul ruined it by saying: "Yeah, you would make a great cheerleader!"

Everyone laughed. I laughed with them to show that I could take a joke, but I felt like it kind of took away some of the cool points I'd earned with Chelsea.

"Yeah, Josh. You'd make a great mascot," she said and flashed me a dazzling smile.

Somehow that didn't sound so bad, after all.

We all ran as fast as we could to the Aviary. It was a sight to behold. All the monkeys were in there except the Colonel and they were all up to no good.

"Those poor birds," Chelsea said.

The monkeys were running around and pulling on the tail feathers of all the big birds. And for no other reason except orneriness.

"We have to stop them!" Marina exclaimed.

"But how?" Manny asked.

"Let's charge them!" Eddie offered.

We all looked at each other and nodded. We started running towards them. What happened next, could have never been predicted. One of the smaller monkeys reached behind his bottom and flung something in our direction. It went sailing high and landed right in front of Eddie. We all looked down in amazement. We could hear laughter coming from that monkey, or at least it sounded like laughter.

"Oh, my gosh! Is that what I think it is?" Bria asked.

Eddie bravely bent over to see and yelled, "POOP! It's poop. This is WAR!"

Eddie's loud war cry seemed to make the monkeys angrier. Now they were all throwing their poop at us. A huge one flew right by my ear. Not only could I hear it whiz by, but I could smell it too. Ew! Manny ducked just in time to miss a barrage of poop flying in his direction. We all started backing away except for Eddie. Always ready for the *what if's*, Eddie pulled a catcher's mask out of his backpack. He threw off his hat and replaced with the mask. Then he grabbed a tree branch, broke it off and yelled, "I need light, shine on me!" We all turned in his direction. He used the tree branch as a bat and hit the poop back at the monkeys. Genius!

The monkeys ganged up and were targeting Eddie. All the poop was now directed at him and only him. Eddie was swinging away like it was the bottom of the ninth and the bases were loaded!

"Guys, some help!" he pleaded.

We scrambled and grabbed tree branches for bats. Marina ran over and grabbed Eddie's hat off the ground and placed it on his head so he could have a light. He looked like some bizarre baseball playing, coal miner.

"Thanks, Marina!" Eddie said. He swatted away a huge turd that went sailing so high it would have been considered a homerun anywhere but here.

I swung as hard as I could but to no avail. I kept striking out. All the evidence lay at my feet; a huge, stinking pile of monkey poop. Paul and Manny were doing much better than me. They were actually hitting some of the poop balls with their branch bats. The girls weren't doing as well because instead of using their branches as baseball bats, they were using them as shields from the poop that was being hurled at them. We were screaming and the monkeys were screaming; all in all, a very impressive sight.

"Retreat! Retreat!" Eddie commanded.

"We are!" Paul screamed back.

"Hey, maybe I should go out for baseball," Manny said to no one in particular.

Ewws and eeks were all I could hear from the girls.

One of the bigger monkeys was preparing to throw a big poop turd straight for Manny. The monkey was winding up his arm like he was a pitcher on a mound, holding the turd ever so carefully, but Manny was ready for the pitch. He was in a batter's stance like he was at home plate. He was twirling the tree branch in his hand just waiting to make contact with the spinning turd. We stopped what we were doing to watch. All our lights lit him up like a stage spotlight.

"I, I, I got it!" Manny yelled as he swung with all his might.

It was as if time stood still. Manny's world class swing made direct contact with the turd, emitting a loud WHACK!

"Perfect," Eddie said.

"Straight shot," Paul added.

"Gross," Marina muttered.

"Awesome," was all I could say.

Our eyes followed the turd as it arched through the night sky and travelled straight back to where the monkey stood.

BULLS-EYE! It landed smack on the monkey's face. Dead center! Manny couldn't have planned it better if he tried. We all held our breaths, anticipating how the monkey would react. He slowly wiped the excrement from his face. His eyes were wild.

"We might have gone too far with these primates. You know they're used to being the kings of the jungle," I said.

"I think lions are the kings of the jungle," Paul added.

"Actually, you are both wrong. Lions don't live in the jungle, they live in the Savannah.

It's a popular mistake because lions are at the top of the food chain," Eddie said.

"I wish we were at the top of the food chain right now," I said.

The monkeys had gathered in a small group and were staring at us.

"Another interesting fact is that the King of Sparta was named King Leonidas and his name meant lion-like. That's why people think that lions are the…"

"Not now Eddie, they're getting closer," I whispered, interrupting his history lesson.

The monkeys were slowly inching their way toward us. There were five in all: two males, two females and little baby Chortles, clinging to his mama .Still no Colonel, and that made me nervous.

Eddie pondered this new information for a moment and said, "Let's all stand real close together. It might be worse than we thought."

"Yes, we need to look formidable." Marina added.

"Really, Marina? You can't use plain English right now. We might be under attack any minute," Eddie said.

"Fine! We need to look intimidating. Is that better, Eddie?"

Eddie puffed out his chest. "That's what I'm talking about!"

We followed Eddie's lead and puffed out our chests, too. The girls stood tall with their hands on their hips.

Eddie let out a tremendous yell, then Paul, then Manny and then me. Mine seemed a little more higher pitched than the others.

Eddie put his hands over his ears. "Really, Josh, you scream like a girl."

It was working. The monkeys started backing away. "Keep screaming Josh, they hate the sound of your girlie voice," Eddie yelled.

I kept screaming, I didn't care how girlie I sounded. The more I screamed, the farther they backed away.

"Let them have it, Josh," Chelsea said.

She didn't have to tell me twice. I started waving my arms around and stomping my feet just like I saw them do. I raised my screams to an even higher level and it worked. It really worked. Not only did the monkeys back away they actually turned and started running away from us. They made a quick escape out of the Aviary and left us standing in amazement.

"Three cheers for Josh!" Paul said.

But before they could cheer for me, I said, "Well, it was really Manny who started their retreat. It was that great hit that landed on that monkey's face."

"Like they say: When you're right, you're right," Eddie said as he lifted Manny onto his shoulders, just like at the end of World Series Games, where the most valuable player gets hoisted up before the team.

Everyone was chanting, "Manny! Manny!"

Darn, I kinda wished it were me. My throat hurt from all that screaming. Chelsea laid her hand on my shoulder and looked right in my eyes.

"Great job, Josh," was all she said.

I was a hero, even if it was only in my own mind.

CHAPTER 11

We all sat in the middle of the Aviary trying hard to catch our breath from the Great Poop Battle, as Eddie was calling it. We were passing around Eddie's water canteen that he borrowed from the gift shop. We took turns sipping greedily. Eddie pulled a map of the zoo out of his right front vest pocket followed by a black permanent marker from his left front vest pocket.

"I got this map from the gift shop, thought it might come in handy," he said. "Now as I see it, the zoo can be broken up into four quadrants: first, the Aviary, which we already checked and cleared," he said as he drew a big X through the Aviary with the black marker. "That just leaves The Petting Zoo, Big Cat Country and Bear Woods, which of course leads to Alligator Alley. We should split up into three groups."

"Us girls will take the Petting Zoo," Marina said.

"I'll check Big Cat Country," Paul said.

"I'll check the Petting Zoo, too," Manny said.

"Manny and I will check Big Cat Country," Paul said glaring at Manny.

Manny looked a little scared, but shrugged his shoulders in agreement.

"That just leaves Bear Woods and Alligator Alley for us, Josh," Eddie said.

Great, the scariest ones.

"We'll check our designated areas and then check in with each other using these walkie-talkies. They're a little bit primitive compared to cell phones, but they'll do the trick." Eddie added, "That's how they communicate in the zoo. Now we're like real Junior Zookeepers," he said proudly.

Marina had one and so did Paul.

"So what, we just check our area and then say it's clear?" Marina asked.

"Ah, no. First, you scout the area as you approach it. You know, to make sure nothing is lurking in the shadows. Then you check the area real slow like. Then you say 'All Clear, from the Red Spy Team', and then you say 'over'."

"Who's the Red Spy Team?' Marina asked.

"There is no Red Spy Team."

"Then why'd you say it? Anyway, I thought we were Junior Zookeepers, not junior spies," Marina said.

She could be so literal at times.

"We are. We are Junior Zookeepers with a mission to spy on the animals and make sure they are okay. It makes perfect sense," Eddie said.

Marina rolled her eyes.

"Now, we all need to pick a 'handle' or spy team name to check in with each other."

"And that's the best you could come up with? Red Spy Team?" Marina interjected. She must really hate spies or the color red, or both.

"Marina is right. We do need cool team names," Manny added.

"I agree. How about the Monkey Avengers, Team 1, 2 and 3?" Eddie asked. "Of course Josh and I would be Monkey Avenger Team #1 or M.A.T. #1 for short."

"MAT? That's a boy's name and we're girls. We want a girl's name!" Marina insisted.

"I agree with the girls," I said.

"What? You want a girl's name for our team?" Eddie recoiled in horror.

"No. I mean I agree that the name should be something real cool. Not Red Spy Team or M.A.T."

"Well, what do you suggest?" Eddie said.

"Everyone knows the real way to find your spy name is to combine your favorite cartoon character with your favorite cereal." I said, feeling very creative.

"That's super cool!" Manny said. "I love Snoopy!" he announced proudly.

"I love Rice Chex!" Paul added.

"Really? You are going to be the Snoopy Rice Chex?" Eddie said. "It sounds a little bit girlie."

"I also like Spiderman." Manny said.

"He's an action hero, not a cartoon," Paul said.

"Actually, he really is both." I added, my geekiness showing.

"Spiderman is too long for a spy handle. Think short names." Eddie said.

"So I guess Clifford the Big Red Dog is out? What about Casper the Friendly Ghost?" I asked.

"Uh, yeah. What if you're in a crisis situation and you only have a few seconds to get out a couple of words. You will be wasting words just on your spy handle. You need to keep it short."

"Okay, good point. How about Garfield?" I added. I thought he was funny.

"Not bad," Eddie said.

"And you like Cheerios!"

"Garfield Cheerios? Naw, they're both too round. Spies are sleek, not fat."

We spent several minutes coming up with combinations of cartoons and cereals. Here were some of the ones we came up with: Boo-Boo Wheaties, Goofy Apple Jacks, Cartman Cocoa Puffs, Honeycomb Tweeties, Stewie Kix, Homer-Pops, Shaggy Rice Krispies, and Scooby Doo Special K's.

After settling on our spy team names, we checked our new zoo watches, provided by the gift shop, temporarily of course, and decided to meet back at the Tree House in one hour.

We were on the move. The girls headed south and made their way toward the Petting Zoo. Manny and Paul headed north towards Big Cat Country. Both teams had a very short distance to walk to begin their search. Eddie and I had the farthest to go just to start ours. We followed Manny and Paul part of the way and then skirted past them. We were headed for the north side of Monkey Island, where the kayak station was located.

Once we reached our destination, Eddie began creeping slowly around the area like he was a soldier sneaking up on an enemy. He looked at me and made a bizarre series of hand gestures that would have confused even a four star general. I shrugged because I didn't understand. He repeated the signs again.

Eddie put his hands to his eyes, and then panned them around the area. He pointed to his ear and mimicked an old person trying to hear. Then he did this weird thing where he pretended to peel a banana and eat it. Then he pointed to Bear Woods. Lastly, he made a little walking motion with two of his fingers across the palm of his other hand. I shrugged again. After three more times of the same pantomime, he finally gave up and spoke as he made the signs.

"I looked around," he said pointing to his eyes and then panning his fingers around the area. "And then I listened for the monkeys in the bush," he said as he made the old person trying to hear gesture. "I didn't see or hear any monkeys around," he said as he peeled a banana and took a bite. "So, let's walk to Bear Woods," he said pointing to Bear Woods and made his two fingers walk across his palm.

"Oh!" I said. It did make sense after he explained it.

"You would make a terrible soldier, Josh," Eddie said.

"I don't think those are real soldier gestures."

"Ah, I'm pretty sure they are. I've definitely seen the eye one in movies."

"Okay, I'll give you that one. But I don't think the banana one is real."

"Sure it is! Everyone knows that one."

"Come on, Eddie. I'm not buying it. What soldier would use an 'eating a banana' gesture while scoping out the enemy?"

"See Josh, you're assuming the enemy is always a man. But the truth is, there are many animal enemies that soldiers are responsible for keeping at bay."

"Name one monkey that we have ever been at war with."

"Ah, I'll name several. Let's see, there is Bigfoot, the Abominable Snowman, and the Swamp Ape…"

"Hold on! We have never been at war with those creatures."

"Don't be so sure. I heard on this underground podcast how Bigfoot along with the Abominable Snowman were planning to attack the gift shop at the top of Pike's Peak in

Colorado. See, they were mad because people kept moving to the Rocky Mountains, which everybody knows is Bigfoot territory."

"First of all, there is no Bigfoot."

"You know that's not true. Remember that photograph I showed you on the Internet? It was of a Bigfoot crossing sign just like a deer crossing sign. But instead of a deer silhouette, it had a Bigfoot silhouette. And it was in the Rocky Mountain National Park on the way up to Pike's Peak."

Eddie was right. There really was a Bigfoot crossing sign on the way up Pike's Peak. He made a good argument, but I wasn't ready to let it go.

"What about the Abominable Snowman? He lives in Alaska, not in Colorado," I said triumphantly.

"Duh, Josh. Everyone knows that. But what they don't know is that there is an un-written code of the big man-apes that states when a brother man-ape is in trouble, that his cousin man-ape must come to his defense."

"How in the world would a person even know that?"

"Simple. The guy who was broadcasting the podcast was a soldier who disguised himself as a Bigfoot and lived with a group of Bigfoot, undercover like. You know, just to gather information about them. He was the one who came up with the banana peeling gesture for all man-apes."

I had to agree that did sound plausible, but then I had another thought. "Um Eddie, where do bananas grow?"

"I dunno. Hot climates I think."

"Aha! Your story is flawed! How would a Bigfoot, who lives in the Rockies, even know what a banana looks like? It's way too cold to grow bananas in the mountains!"

"There is a really good story that explains that too, but we don't have time for it right now," he said as we approached the entrance to Bear Woods.

We both tip-toed as quietly as we could to the first cage. It said "Sloth Bears." They were up and about.

"Look at the baby one. It's riding on its mom's back," I said to Eddie.

"Cool," Eddie said.

When the little cub heard us, it burrowed down and hid in its mom's fur. "They do that when they are scared," Eddie said.

"Ah, we aren't going to hurt you," I said through the bars.

"It doesn't know that. To him, we are huge bear-eating things," Eddie said.

"I guess."

"This is team Butthead Wheaties. We just checked the sloth bear cage. All clear. Over and out," Eddie said into the walkie-talkie.

"This is team Sponge Bob Square Pants Peanut Butter Toast Crunch, we just checked out the bear cat cage and they are fine. By the way, the bear cats look nothing like bears or cats. A little disappointing. Over and out," Paul said.

"They really should rethink that spy name," Eddie said.

"I like it," I said. "I wonder what the bear cats look like." I pictured cats that looked like bears. "Maybe we should check on the girls."

"Team Dora Honey Smacks, do you read?" Eddie asked.

"This is team Dora Honey Smacks. We are fine. They have the cutest animals in the Petting Zoo. They are so friendly. We are feeding them right now. So far no signs of monkeys. Over and out," Marina answered.

"I wish we would have gotten the Petting Zoo. We could be feeding cute animals right now."

"Really, Josh. There are monkeys hiding in the zoo somewhere and it's up to us to find them. You would rather pet and feed girlie animals?" Eddie said, looking straight at me.

"Um, no, but…"

"But what? This is far better than any planned overnight field trip. We are really on an adventure," Eddie reminded me.

"Yeah, I guess so. I just don't want any trouble."

"What trouble could we possibly have? We are just going to round up the monkeys and put them back on Monkey Island and then enjoy the rest of the night in the Tree House. It's as simple as that."

But I knew that nothing was ever as simple as Eddie thought.

We spent an hour checking out Bear Woods and Alligator Alley. Everything seemed in its place. We checked back and forth between the teams and they were reporting the same thing. All clear and no monkeys. Where could they be hiding?

"Maybe they all went back to Monkey Island?" I said.

"Well, it would make sense. That is their home. Maybe they got bored and wanted to head home," Eddie said.

"It's just about time to head back to our home base," I reminded Eddie.

Eddie checked his watch, "Yep, let's head back."

"This is the final check in from team Butt-head Wheaties. All clear and heading back to the Tree House. Over and out," Eddie told them.

"We read you loud and clear, Buttheads. This is Team Dora Honey Smacks," Marina said. We could hear laughter in the background. "We just finished playing with, I mean checking on the animals. Ah, there's that cute donkey. He's heading right to me. We will start heading over there..." Their radio went dead.

"Did she call us buttheads? It's team Butt-head Wheaties. And she forgot to say over and out." Eddie fumed.

"Yeah, she did call us buttheads and she did forget to say over and out. Do you think they're okay?" I asked.

"Yeah, they're probably taking turns riding on the donkey." Eddie saw my expression and continued, "Don't worry, Josh. I will make sure we get back to the Petting Zoo again before we leave."

"Thanks, Eddie."

He just rolled his eyes. "Team Sponge Bob Square Pants Peanut Butter Toast Crunch, do you read me?"

"Grunt." Was all we heard.

"Are you guys heading back to the tree house now?"

"Grunt, grunt."

Eddie and I looked at each other. "That was weird," I said.

"I thought so too. Are they too lazy to answer us?" Eddie asked.

Eddie yelled into the walkie-talkie, "Hey guys, are you heading back now? Over and out."

"Grunt, grunt, grunt."

Eddie stared at the walkie-talkie. "I guess that means yes."

"I guess so, let's roll.".

CHAPTER 12

As Eddie and I were heading back to the Tree House, he started talking to me. I mean really talking.

"Do you think Marina is mad at me?" he asked.

Whoa, where did that come from? Eddie never cared who was mad at him, especially a girl. "Um, why do you care?" I asked.

"It's not that I care, it's just that she does have some good ideas, but mine are better. She's really smart. I, I just…"

"You have a crush on her, don't you?" I couldn't believe it.

"What? No! That's just crazy, Josh!" Eddie playfully pushed me. I fell to the ground.

"Ouch!" I said. Eddie didn't know his own strength.

"Sorry, I forgot you were so wimpy." Eddie flexed his muscles. "I might go out for football next year. What do you think?"

"I think I wouldn't want you coming at me at full speed." I was telling the truth.

"Thanks, Josh."

"It wasn't a compliment."

"This is Team Butthead Wheaties, come in Team Dora and Sponge Bob. Over." Eddie paced nervously back and forth in the Canopy Café. "I don't like this, Josh. They were supposed to be here fifteen minutes ago."

I didn't want to agree with Eddie, but well, I agreed with Eddie. Something did feel very wrong.

"I think our best bet is to stay put and wait just a little longer," I said not eager to go back out there with the Colonel running loose.

"One of us could stay while the other does recognizance."

"Not a good idea, Eddie. We only have one walkie-talkie. How would we communicate?"

I was grateful he had forgotten that there was a room full of walkie-talkies located in the administrative offices. "Excellent point," he said.

"Still, we need to find out what's going on. Follow me," he said, and went out on the balcony.

Eddie looked through the night vision binoculars. "We need to scan the entire zoo. See if we can see them. We'll start here, facing Monkey Island and we'll walk around the balcony clockwise, towards Big Cat Country. These binoculars will pick up any movement, no matter how small."

"So, they are good enough to pick up a monkey?"

"Yes."

"Then why didn't we all just stay up here and scan the zoo from the safety of the Tree House before?"

Eddie's face fell. I could tell that thought had never crossed his mind. He tried to play it off. "Well it's complicated. And there's no time to explain," he stammered.

Eddie began scanning the area while I tried to get a reply on the walkie-talkies.

"Big Cat Country looks clear…Wait! I see movement! Yes. It looks like Paul and Manny are running. Really hard. Something big must be after them! Probably a lion!"

I grabbed the binoculars from Eddie's head and peered through them. I saw Manny and Paul in a flat out run. I looked behind them, fully expecting to see a lion in hot pursuit, but I saw nothing. That is until I looked up. High up in the trees was a tribe of monkeys in full swing. They were chasing them from the tree tops.

"It's the monkeys!" I screamed.

Eddie grabbed the binoculars back and confirmed what I saw. We ran around the balcony of the Canopy Café to keep up with Paul and Manny's progress through the zoo.

"They reached the Petting Zoo!" Eddie breathed hard. "The girls just met them."

"What do you see?"

"Um…lots of hand gestures. Good thing I'm good at reading them. Let's see, Marina is flapping her hands and pointing to the don-key. So the donkey must be in on it."

"That can't be right," I said.

Eddie held up his hand in a silence gesture. "Now Manny and Paul are practically shoving the girls forward. I think they want them to move."

"Duh, they're being chased by crazy, feral primates."

"Now they're all running," he said and I continued to follow him around the balcony. Thank goodness the balcony went around the whole café.

Eddie watched as they passed the entrance of the zoo. They flew through Alligator Alley and Bear Woods. Finally, they approached Monkey Island.

"No! They're in a fight for their lives!" Eddie screamed.

I couldn't take it anymore. I snatched the binoculars from Eddie's hands. What I saw made my blood run cold. My friends had run all the way to Monkey Island and they were using the kayak paddles as make-shift weapons. They were poking and stabbing the air to try to keep the monkeys at bay. The monkeys were throwing poop at them. Ew.

Eddie snatched the goggles back.

"What's going on?" I asked.

"They have their backs against the water. One of the girls, maybe Marina, is walking backwards on the fallen log across the river. She's yelling something. I can't make it out, but it looks like she's trying to tell them to follow her."

Even in a crisis she's bossy, I thought to myself.

"Now both teams are following her over the log. They're on the island! The monkeys are backing off a bit. Genius! They're working together to push the log into the water. They did it! Now the monkeys can't cross the river! They're safe!"

"Except now they're trapped."

Eddie looked at me with a crooked smile. "Then it's up to us to save them."

I'd never seen Eddie so worked up. He was pacing back and forth and mumbling to himself. I picked up the binoculars and stared. True enough, the gang was safe on Monkey Island. However, the monkeys were going crazy. And then I saw him, the Colonel! He looked right up at me and pointed. I dropped Eddie's binoculars.

"Dude, careful, those are expensive." Eddie said.

"The Colonel just saw me and pointed at me," I told him.

"No way. We are too far away and it's dark. You are just seeing things."

"I know what I saw. He's after me."

"Oh, yeah, that I believe, but first we have to save everyone, then we can worry about the Colonel getting you," Eddie explained.

"How are we going to save everyone?" I asked.

"I can only come up with one solution and you aren't going to like it."

I already knew that.

My stomach ached and my legs shook. Small beads of sweat trickled down my forehead. I looked over at Eddie. He was as calm as a cucumber as he grabbed his backpack.

We stepped out to the balcony. The night air felt cool and helped calm me down a bit. Eddie was double checking our harnesses.

"Safety first, I always say," Eddie said as he pulled on my line to verify its hold. "Ready, Josh?"

All I could do was nod my head 'yes.' I can't believe we were getting ready to zip-line down to Monkey Island. And not all the way down exactly. We had to jump off before the end so we would land right in the middle of the island. Eddie was going first.

"Alright, I'm getting ready to swing out. You follow sixty seconds after me. That's one minute. You can time it exactly right by saying Mississippis."

"Why do I have to wait? Why can't I go at the same time you go?" I asked. We were on two parallel zip-lines. Part of me was afraid that if I saw him go, I might not follow.

"Because if we went at the same time you wouldn't know when to jump off at the exact time."

"Huh?" I said.

"I know precisely where to drop, you don't. And if I go first, I can drop and then you will have time to drop where I did," he said.

"Yeah, that makes sense," I said nervously.

"Josh, look at me," Eddie requested.

I did.

"You need to stop shaking. Do you see me shaking?"

I didn't. Eddie showed no fear. He was in his element. "No, you are as steady as a rock," I told him and he was.

"Well, technically there are some rocks that aren't steady. In Death Valley National Park, there is a place called Racetrack Playa. It is this dried up lake that is surrounded by mountains. It's made up of pebbles, rock, and big boulders. The really interesting thing is that there are lines on the ground that show that these rocks move and leave trails; like they are racing each other."

"Really, Eddie? Right now, you're going to give me a lecture on rocks that aren't steady?" I was close to chickening out, but the thought of our friends stuck on Monkey Island kept me focused. I didn't have time to comprehend this frivolous information Eddie was giving me about rocks. I put on my gloves, hoping this would stop him from talking. It didn't.

"It's just that it is really weird because there are no humans there and the wind can't do it. So, the theory is that maybe aliens or some sort of creature that hasn't been discovered yet flies down and skis on them. You know, leaving the rock trails. Or maybe the aliens are racing each other on them. Anyway, these rocks are anything but steady. Instead, you should say steady as a lock. Locks are super steady. That's how they keep things out, or should I say keep things in. Their steadiness." Eddie finally stopped talking and put on his gloves. "Just trying to get your mind off what we are about to do." He smiled and swung out. "Start counting! Bombs away!" Eddie disappeared into the dark night. I could hear him 'woo-hooing' as he zipped away.

"One Mississippi, two Mississippi, three Mississippi…" It was no use. All I could think about was aliens racing each other. Darn it, Eddie. But it was too awesome not to think about it. "Okay, this is it." I grabbed on the line and pushed off. I knew instantly my yells were not near as cool as Eddie's woohoo's. I sounded like a scared little girl again.

The wind whipped through my hair and my stomach dropped like I was on a rollercoaster, plummeting down, down, down. I watched

Eddie in front of me, way in front of me. He weighed a lot more than me, so he went faster on the zip-line.

He was just over Monkey Island when he started slowing down a bit because the rope began leveling off. When he was about six feet from the ground, he released the harness, hit the ground on the soft shore with bent knees and tucked and rolled. He got up and ran farther into the island. Then he pulled out a couple of flashlights and began frantically waving them at me like I was a plane taxiing down the runway.

I felt my momentum slow as I neared the island. I started fiddling with the harness to release and drop in the same spot as Eddie did.

"Jump now!" Eddie yelled. He frantically waved to the spot with the flashlights.

I couldn't get the harness loose. I pulled and pulled the carabineer clip to release my harness from the cable, but it didn't work. I began panicking. I was almost over the shore and headed right for Eddie.

"Stop screwing around and jump!" Eddie screamed.

I kept pulling the clip, but couldn't get it to release. "Look out!" I screamed as I blew past the shore and headed for the grass, right where Eddie was standing. Finally, I remembered that you had to push the clip to release it. I pushed and yanked the harness out and found myself in a free fall.

I must have fallen for five minutes. How did I get so high? I felt like I was falling from an airplane like a paratrooper, or I was falling down a large elevator shaft. I didn't think I would ever stop. Finally, I hit the ground with a thud.

Eddie laughed uproariously. Somehow, our friends had joined him. They must have had time to gather around while I was free falling for several minutes. They all stood around me in a circle.

I laid on my back with the wind knocked out of me. I couldn't figure out what was so funny about the death defying stunt I had just pulled off.

"What's so funny?" I asked, after I got my breath back.

"Ah, I dunno. Just that you screamed like a little girl all the way down the zip-line." Eddie chuckled.

"I did?" I asked. "Well, you would too if you fell several hundred feet from the air!"

"Stand up, Josh," Eddie said giving me his hand to help me up.

I stood up and my hair got tangled into

something above my head. It was the harness dangling from the zip-line. I guess I had only fallen a few feet instead of several hundred. I dusted the dirt off my bottom and turned bright red. Thankfully no one could tell because of the dark.

CHAPTER 13

"**I remember seeing** a small shack on a map in the administrative offices. It's located on the east side of the island. We'll find the door that leads to the underground chunnel, back to the Tree House," Eddie said as he pulled a com-pass out of his vest pocket and shone the flashlight on it.

The island was kind of spooky at night. We followed Eddie in a single file line as he made his way to the east side of the island.

"That was brave of you to use the zip-line to come save us," Chelsea whispered behind me.

"It was nothing," I said and turned bright red again.

Eddie held up his fist to signal *stop*. "It's straight ahead," he whispered covertly.

"Why are we whispering?" Marina asked in a whisper.

"I don't know," he answered in a whisper, and then repeated it in a more manly voice, "I mean, I don't know," he said loudly.

The shack was just that; a concrete square building with a solid metal door and one small window set very high.

Eddie tried the door and found it locked. "Locked. We're gonna have to break in. I've got a plan."

Eddie reached into a vest pocket and pulled out his ABC gum wad and then he pulled some firecrackers from his backpack. "I will secure the firecrackers to the lock using this gum. Then I'll light the fuse and we'll all run for the hills."

"What hills?" I asked.

"It's just an expression that means to run really fast away from the explosion, duh."

"Oh."

"Here's the bad part. The gum has been sitting for a while so it got all hardened up. There's too much for me to soften on my own, so everyone will have to chew some to get it soft again."

"Eeeew!" all three girls said at once and I agreed.

"Men, we can't expect the girls to help. You know…girl cooties and all." Eddie said as he divided the gum into four chunks. He handed each of us a chuck. Manny popped his into his mouth and began chewing quickly.

"Not bad," he said with a full mouth. "I think it was grape."

"It was," Eddie mumbled back.

Paul looked a little sick to his stomach, but he chewed reluctantly. The girls were staring at us with mouths agape. I popped the ABC gum into my mouth and told myself it was a nice, new, unchewed piece of gum so I would not throw up. I didn't want to be the only boy not to man up in front of the girls, especially after my super girlie scream.

We chewed for a while and then Eddie collected the gum. I happily spit mine into his hand. He fastened the firecrackers to the key-hole with the gum and lit the fuse. We all ran for the hills, just like we were in a war movie escaping a grenade. We ducked behind a big log, covering our heads to protect ourselves from exploding door fragments.

A few moments later, we heard a very small pop. I looked at Eddie and he shrugged.

"Seems like it would have been louder," he whispered.

"Yeah, let's take a look," I answered.

We crept forward cautiously. Our faces fell when we viewed the door. It looked like the keyhole had tried to blow the world's biggest bubble and succeeded. The door was covered in gum, but the lock held steady.

"Steady as a lock," Eddie sighed.

"If only we had the key," I said.

"Oh my gosh, guys! We do have the key!" Marina said.

"We do?" I asked.

"Yes. Eddie does. Remember when you took the keys from Hog? I'm sure one of them was a master key," she said.

Eddie dug in his pockets and produced Hog's keys. He walked to the door and tried to put the biggest key into the keyhole.

"It won't go. It's all jammed up with bubblegum," he said deflated.

"Alright Bria, it's up to us," Chelsea said.

Bria nodded like she knew what Chelsea was talking about. Bria and Chelsea walked around to the side of the shack and stood underneath the window. Bria bent her leg and Chelsea expertly climbed from the crook in Bria's thigh to her shoulder. Chelsea grabbed Bria's hands and stood up like she did it every day. I recognized it as a cheerleading move. Chelsea was standing on Bria's shoulders, and Bria was holding the back of Chelsea's legs to keep her steady. Bria moved right under the window as petite Chelsea scrambled through. A moment later, Chelsea stood in front of the open door grinning happily.

"Let's go!' she said.

I smiled at her, my new heroine.

A moment later, we were all creeping down the chunnel. It was a long concrete tunnel with reflective lights set into the floor. It was still kinda dark and felt really eerie. It reminded me of the fallout shelter in one of my video games. Gray and cold. No one really spoke when we were walking, like any noise might wake up a ghost or a killer robot just around the corner. I shivered.

Finally we reached the door to the Tree House, but this time Eddie did use the master key to open it. Everyone sighed as we crossed the threshold into the dark, but secure Tree House lobby.

"Okay. Safe and sound. Now let's all head back to the Canopy Café to formulate our next move," Eddie said.

"Next move? Our next move should be to go to our rooms, snuggle into our sleeping bags and wake up when this nightmare is over," I said.

Paul, Bria and Marina nodded their heads in agreement.

"Negative," Eddie said. "We still have to secure the monkeys, and then we can rest. To the Canopy Café." He pointed dramatically up the stairs. I reluctantly followed.

When we reached the Canopy Café, Eddie popped into the walk-in cooler as we lit some candles on the table. Eddie came out of the cooler with an enormous strawberry cake in one hand and a jug of milk in the other.

"Okay troops," he said as he placed the cake on the table. "Everyone knows an army moves on its stomach."

"So you brought us some cake?" Marina asked as she cut the cake and put it on paper plates for everyone.

"What do you mean?"

"You said an army moves on its stomach, so you brought us cake to fill our stomachs. Right?" she asked.

"Uh, no. I just thought some cake sounded good, but just to be clear, that's not what that expression means. It means that soldiers have to crawl around on their stomachs so the enemy can't see them. That's why they teach you to crawl on your belly underneath barbed

139

wire in basic training. So we need to make a plan that involves moving stealthily on our stomachs."

"An army moves on its stomach means that you have to feed the soldiers so they can stay strong and healthy. In other words, you need food for energy so you can fight," she said as she helped herself to some strawberry cake and a cold glass of milk.

Eddie looked puzzled.

"I wish I had some chocolate cake." I said knowing it would bug Eddie to think of it after the incident earlier this year when he gobbled up half a chocolate cake.

"I have a chocolate bar in my backpack," Manny said and began rummaging around in his backpack.

He pulled his hand out quickly and gave a startled cry. We all turned to look.

"What is it?" I asked.

"There's something furry in there, and it moved!" He shivered.

"Alright, don't panic," Eddie said. "Josh, go take a look and I'll watch your back."

"What? Why me?"

"Because you have small hands and they fit better into the backpack."

"I do not!"

"Okay, fine. I'll do it," Eddie said.

Just then, I looked at Chelsea and suddenly got brave. "Wait, I'll do it. But not because I have little hands, which I don't."

I cautiously walked over to Manny's backpack. Everyone turned their helmet lights on me to help me see.

I tried to peer in at first, but couldn't see anything. I opened the backpack and peered in. Something moved! I jumped back a little and everyone behind me jumped a little, too.

"There's something in there. Manny was right." I said breathlessly.

"What is it?" Eddie asked nervously.

"Be careful not to hurt it!" Marina added.

"Yes, Josh. Be very careful. We don't know what's in there and it could bite you," Eddie added.

"Thanks a lot," I said, as I screwed up my courage to have another look.

"Or it could be poisonous," he added.

That did it. Courage gone. Hello chicken.

Just then, Chelsea passed right by me and reached into the backpack. She let out a little "Aw" as she pulled out a baby patas monkey. It was Chortles, the monkey we had all helped to name.

Chortles leapt out of Chelsea's arms and crawled up my leg. He wedged himself firmly in the crook of my arm and nestled his head into my chest.

"He likes you," she said. He certainly appeared to have taken a shine to me.

"Maybe, you remind him of his mother," Eddie said and everyone laughed.

"That's it!" Paul screamed.

"What? Josh is a monkey's mother?" Eddie was still laughing.

"No, that's why the monkeys were chasing us. We had their baby and they wanted him back," Paul said. "The monkeys even took our walkie-talkie."

That explains the grunts Eddie and I heard coming from their walkie-talkie.

"We lost our walkie-talkie too," Marina said.

"The donkey accidentally stepped on it," Bria explained.

"That still doesn't explain the baby monkey," Eddie said.

"Yeah, that's weird. How did it get in my backpack?" Manny asked.

"Oh, I know how! Remember when we were checking Big Cat Country and you were gathering all those bananas because you said that you could fry them for us later in the kitchen. You said they were called planktons. Maybe the baby was watching you and wanted those bananas for himself," Paul reminded Manny.

"What? You were going to serve us fried planktons? That's crazy? You can't eat plank-tons. They are tiny micro-organisms that live in water. Why would you do that?" Marina asked angrily.

"Yeah, not cool, Manny," Eddie chimed in.

"I thought Plankton was the mean guy on SpongeBob. Isn't he?" Chelsea asked.

"Yes, he is. Why were you going to serve us the mean guy?" Paul asked.

"Mean guy or sea micro thingies, either way still not cool Manny." Eddie summed up what everyone was feeling.

Manny was silent. He looked a little hurt, but also a little confused.

"Do you have something to say to us, Manny?" Marina asked.

Manny cleared his throat and said, "I'm not sure what to say. I never said plankton. I said plantains. They are like big bananas. My nana used to make them for us all the time. They are really tasty. I thought you guys would like them."

"Oh, that does sound good!" Eddie said. "Are you still going to do it? Because I could eat some right now."

"Eddie, no! We have more pressing problems!" Marina exclaimed.

They all looked at me. Chortles was sleeping peacefully in the crook of my arm. Little snores were emitting from his tiny body.

"You're right, Marina. We need a new plan. One that involves giving the baby back to the monkeys," Eddie said.

"Yes, you're right, Eddie," Marina said. Everyone looked at her. This might be one of the first times Marina and Eddie agreed with each other right away. "If we give the baby back, the monkeys will retreat."

"True, but we have to do much more than that. We have to make sure each and every monkey is safe and secure back on Monkey Island." Eddie added.

"Wait a minute. We don't have to do that. We just have to give the baby back. Then our problems are solved with the monkeys. You just want to keep this adventure going, don't you?" Marina asked Eddie.

"So you admit it's an adventure? I knew it. I knew this was an adventure. Probably the greatest one we have ever had, huh, Josh?" He looked in my direction.

I was afraid to respond.

Marina looked away in disgust. Her agreement with Eddie was over as fast as it started.

I guess I needed to say something that would defuse the situation a bit.

"Maybe we don't have to get them back on the island," I offered.

"I'm listening…," Eddie said.

"What if we just rounded them up somewhere? Somewhere safe, where they would all be together. Would that be okay for everyone?" I said.

Everyone nodded their heads in agreement, except Eddie. He was actually scratching his chin like he was seriously considering it. We were waiting for his response. It was taking forever. Finally, I couldn't take the silence.

"Eddie!" I screamed jarring Eddie from his internal thoughts.

"What?" Eddie said looking straight at me.

"Do you agree or not?"

"Yes, I do. And I know the perfect place to trap them all." Eddie's lips formed an almost sinister smile. Just like an evil genius. Even little Chortles tossed in his sleep.

CHAPTER 14

Eddie strutted around the group as if he were a general addressing his troops.

"As I see it, we need a safe place to contain the monkeys. Not too far and easily accessible. Agreed?" he asked.

"Agreed," we all said in unison.

"I know just the place. Let me take you back to the third grade. The setting? This very zoo. The incident? The Great Banana Revolt. You may remember we visited this zoo on a field trip two years ago to the day!"

"Really?" Marina asked.

"Well, maybe not to the day. But close. Anyway, it was way before Monkey Island was built. Back then the monkeys were kept in what is now known as the old Primate Palace.

We had just finished our bag lunches. Everyone got a banana. As you know, I was on a strict diet of junk food back in those days."

"Yeah, you were kinda big," I said, remembering back to when Eddie was my nemesis and picked on me constantly. Not fun.

He shot me daggers. "Anyway, as I was saying. I wasn't into eating fruit like I am now. By the way Manny, I could really use some of that fried plankton, you know, for fuel for the big monkey capture ahead."

"Plantains." He sighed and then grabbed the plantains out of his backpack. He peeled them and cut them up into one-inch slices. He lit the gas stove with a match and swirled some oil in a pan. He fried the pieces as he listened to Eddie's tale.

"So, I had a banana leftover and thought, monkeys like bananas, right?. So, I saved it in my backpack until we reached the Primate Palace. Remember how it was an open space for the monkeys to run around in? Well, there stood the Colonel. He was a bit younger then, not so much gray in his fine mustache."

"I do remember that? It's weird, but now that you brought it up, I seem to recall someone getting hurt, but who?" Marina asked.

"All in good time," Eddie said lifting his hands up to stop Marina from revealing the end of the story before its time. He really was a good storyteller. I was hooked and I already knew the ending.

"As I stood there looking at our furry friends, I thought they might want a snack. So I wound my arm like a pitcher getting ready to pitch at the World Series, and I let the banana fly like a fastball!"

"Cool!" Manny said, and placed a bunch of hot plantains on a plate. Eddie went to grab one and Manny slapped his hand away. "Not done yet."

Eddie wrung his hand as if it really hurt. "The banana sailed into the Primate Palace like a cannon ball leaving a cannon. It landed squarely at the Colonel's feet. He stood there for a moment eyeballing it; like he was trying to figure out if it was a gift or a curse. I know, because I saw him tug on his mustache."

"So?" I said.

"So, everyone knows when a person tugs on their mustache their thinking hard, duh."

"Yes, every *person*, not every monkey."

"Whatever, Josh. After a few moments, the Colonel picked up the banana and tossed it up and down as if feeling its weight. Then he tossed it from hand to hand. And then he started twirling it like a baton!"

"That never happened!" I yelled.

"Didn't it, Josh? Or did you just block it from your memory after the pain the banana caused when it hit your head?"

I just shook my head.

"I knew the Colonel was going to throw the banana. I just didn't know when. He was toying with me, with all of us. Everyone knew it and started to run. Too late! The banana sailed back across and hit Josh in the back of the head as he was fleeing for his life! He fell to the ground, tearing the flesh from his knees."

"Oh yeah! Now I remember. We all had to go to the first aid station so Josh could get a few Band-Aids for his minor scrapes." Marina said.

"Yeah, we didn't get to see Big Cat Country because of you," Paul added.

"What? Because of me? I'm not the one who threw the banana. Once again, it was Eddie! Blame him not me!"

"I hardly think it's fair to blame me because you got whacked on the back of a head by a banana," he said.

"Agh! You make me crazy! Every time I get hurt or get in trouble, you're not far behind! And by the way, Eddie, why did he hit me and not you?"

Eddie got a very sheepish look on his face.

"I always wondered that! He was a monkey in his prime. He could swing from trees! He could hit a bull's-eye from fifty feet away. Why did he hit me?"

"Alright, calm down. There is a reason, just don't get mad. See, when I first threw the banana, the Colonel wasn't looking at me. He was looking at some of the girl monkeys. Maybe he had a crush on one, I don't know. But his head was turned away. Anyway, when the banana landed at his feet he did look at me, but his gaze was so scary that I pointed at you."

"I knew it! I always knew there was more to the story."

"Enough! Listen to yourselves! Monkeys don't understand pointing and all that other stuff. Get a grip, both of you." Marina said.

"I dunno, it does explain why the Colonel does seem to hate Josh," Manny said. He smashed the fried plantains with the bottom of a glass and then he put them in the oil to fry a second time.

I sat there steaming while Manny placed the plantains on a huge plate for us all to enjoy. He sprinkled powdered sugar over them. I was too mad to try one. Everyone was oohing and aahing about how good they tasted. *Why did Eddie have to ruin everything?*

Now I have a huge monkey on my back and I'm stuck in a "no way out" situation. Maybe it was time I took control.

"Since I'm the one the Colonel is after, I'm now in charge of the rest of this rescue operation," I said as confidently as I could.

"Whoa, wait a minute, Josh! This is my rescue operation," Eddie said getting up from the table.

"Sit down, Eddie. We can take a vote or you can just let me finish talking."

Eddie reluctantly sat down. Now it was his turn to steam a little.

All eyes were on me. I shifted Chortles to my other arm. He was pretty heavy even for a baby monkey. "Okay, since there are seven of us, it would make sense to utilize everyone to their best ability."

I saw many heads nodding in agreement, even Eddie. Eddie raised his hand timidly. I was hesitant to call on him, but then again at least he didn't blurt out what he wanted to say. For Eddie, this was an awesome display of restraint.

"Yes, Eddie," I said.

"What about some sort of system where we could set up different traps along the way leading to the Primate Palace?" Eddie offered.

"That's not a bad idea, actually" Paul said and Manny nodded in agreement.

I looked around the table and realized what an unbelievable group of friends this really was. And that did include Eddie. When we worked together anything was possible, even capturing monkeys. Maybe I was being too hard on Eddie. I really needed his expertise in how to accomplish our goal.

"Does anyone have an idea on how to lure the monkeys to the Primate Palace?" I asked.

"Maybe we could leave a trail of bananas?" Manny said.

"Maybe one of us could dress up like a monkey and lead them there," Paul added.

"Or maybe we could use Chortles as bait to lure them," Marina said.

Chortles held me tighter, like he understood what Marina was saying.

"Maybe we can get some other animals to help us," Chelsea said.

We sat there in silence thinking about all the suggestions. I couldn't help but think they were a little risky and not too probable. How could we possibly get other animals to help us? I didn't like the idea of using Chortles as bait, either. He was so little.

"I got it!" Eddie yelled. "The solution is to combine all of your suggestions!"

"All our ideas?" Marina asked.

"Yep, all of them. The best way to lure the monkeys would be a relay." Eddie proposed.

"You mean like a relay race?" I asked.

"Well, sort of. We set up a trail of bananas at different locations around the zoo. We each play an important part in the relay. Like Josh said earlier, we all have special abilities and we can build on that," Eddie explained.

I was a little proud that Eddie mentioned my earlier statement. "What about using the animals and little Chortles here," I said.

"And who gets to dress up like a monkey?" Paul asked.

"Don't worry; I have answers to all those questions and more. I just need a few minutes to work out all the details in my head." Eddie stood up and paced the floor.

I sat down at Eddie's seat and reached for a plantain. Before I could put it in my mouth, Chortles reached out and grabbed it and popped it into his. He made the cutest sound, almost like a human "yummmm." Everyone laughed. We took turns feeding him plantains. They were really good!

Eddie's plan meant another trek to the gift shop. He really liked the gift shop.

"Okay, I love the idea of using Chortles as bait, but that really wouldn't be very nice or honorable as Junior Zookeepers. So, the next best thing is these furry, little Chortles stuffed animals." Eddie held up the Zoo's newest merchandising ploy, stuffed baby monkeys.

"Oh, they are so cute," Marina cooed.

"I know! I was going to buy one for a souvenir," Chelsea said.

Girls are so weird.

"So Marina and Manny will put a stuffed Chortles in their backpack with the head sticking out. That way, the monkeys will follow them if the banana trail doesn't work. Josh will have the real one and have to do the switch at the end of the relay. I will supervise the relay and make sure that the monkeys follow you all. And in order for me to do that, I will have to wear a monkey mask so I can blend in naturally with the real monkeys," Eddie explained.

I swear I saw Paul sigh with relief. Even though dressing up like a monkey was his idea, I don't think he actually wanted to do it.

We headed into the lobby to listen to the rest of Eddie's plan.

"Well, troops, this is do or die time. Is everyone in?" Eddie asked.

I thought about everything that had happened since we got off the bus earlier this morning. I had already zipped-lined down to Monkey Island, escaped through the chunnel and befriended a baby monkey. *Who knows what else could happen tonight?* I didn't want it to end. "I'm in!" I place my hand in the middle of the group like we had done earlier, hoping to get the same response as last time.

"Me too!" Paul placed his hand on mine.

"Count me in!" Manny's hand went on top of Paul's.

Chelsea, Bria and Marina looked at each other and grinned. "Yep, I'm in," Chelsea said while placing her hand in.

"Same here!" Bria added.

"Me too!" Marina's hand was at the top of the pile.

Eddie was in shock! I think he thought we would all back out. He put his hand on top of Marina's and said, "Junior Zookeepers unite on three: One, two, three!"

"Junior Zookeepers unite!" We yelled in unison. Then we broke our hands away and patted each other's backs like we were at a pep rally or something. It was all very exciting.

"Now back to the plan," Eddie said. "We have a lot to do."

CHAPTER 15

Our plan was all set to go. Looking around the lobby at everyone was truly a sight to see. Marina and Manny had their backpacks on with the little stuffed monkey peeking out of the top. Paul was loaded down with banana bunches. Bria and Chelsea were loaded down with apples and sugar cubes to make sure the donkey, pony and alpaca would let them ride them.

But the best was Eddie. He never ever did things half way. It was always all or nothing with him. He'd taken the giant $100.00 stuffed monkey from the gift shop and carefully cut a slit down its back with his Swiss Army knife. He gingerly removed the stuffing.

"What are you doing?" Marina yelled.

"I'm getting into my character, like those actors who research their roles and never get out of character until the movie is over."

"You mean a method actor?" she asked.

"Nope, don't know him. I can't think of any specific examples right now."

Marina just shook her head.

Eddie cut two slits for the eyes, a hole for his nose and his mouth. Then, he proceeded to climbed into the unstuffed monkey. It fit perfectly.

"Oh my gosh!" Bria exclaimed.

"You'll never get the stuffing back in so it looks the same. You realize that, don't you?" I asked.

He just grunted like a monkey and cocked his head sideways.

"You're going to have to buy that," I said.

Grunt

"It's $100.00."

Grunt.

"That's a lot of money…"

Eddie jumped up and down and scratched under his arm. He moved just like a real monkey. I had no doubt that the monkeys would consider him one of their own.

I just stood there holding Chortles. My job was to stay ahead of everyone on the relay and be the first one to the Primate Palace to give back the baby. Easy enough, right? Then why did my stomach hurt so much?

"Okay, is everyone ready?" Eddie asked us.

We all nodded in agreement, even Chortles was nodding his fuzzy head. I scratched the top of his head and he snuggled into me even more.

"Ahhh, he's so cute," Chelsea said.

"I know! I want to take him home," Marina added.

I stood there blushing like an idiot, even though the comments were for Chortles and not me. Then just as quickly the girls' attention was back on themselves.

"I hope the animals like sugar cubes and apples," Bria said.

"Well, who doesn't?" Eddie volunteered.

It seemed like a good time to start the relay. Everyone was in a good mood as we stepped outside. The moon was huge and it gave us much needed light. It wasn't even scary outside; it was kind of cool, being in the zoo at night with no adults.

The girls gave Chortles little kisses. Paul patted him on the head and Manny tickled him under his chin. Eddie tried to get close, but the closer Eddie got the louder Chortles screamed.

"Stop it, Eddie. You're really scaring him!" Chelsea said.

"Yeah, you look just like the Swamp Ape," Marina said.

Eddie backed off. I couldn't tell if he was upset or not because of his costume.

"Take the costume off. Maybe he'll let you near him them."

Eddie just shook his head. "Nope, can't get out of character. The show must go on!"

That was Eddie. First a soldier and then an actor!

Eddie decided the best way to monitor everyone was to use Hog's golf cart. So we all followed him to the maintenance shed. Eddie fumbled with the keys and unlocked the shed. Emergency lighting flicked on. It was a sight to behold!

"Wow, we should have come here first," I said, eyeing all the goodies inside.

Eddie's monkey face nodded up and down enthusiastically.

Paul ran towards a blue skateboard that was sticking out of a big crate that read, *confiscated stuff*. "This is perfect! Now I can stay ahead of the monkeys."

Manny ran over to see if there was anything that he could use. After rummaging around, he pulled out a pair of inline skates. "I think they are my size." He threw off his shoes and tried them on. "Like a glove!"

Now the girls were pilfering through the crate. They didn't find anything that would help them. "Who would bring firecrackers to a zoo?" Bria asked no one in particular, as she threw them back in the crate. "Oh sorry, Eddie. I forgot you brought some."

"Yes, but I'm out. And you can never have enough!" He ran to the crate with the three of us on his heels. Eddie couldn't see well with the costume on and tripped, but that didn't stop us. We stepped over him to get to the free firecrackers.

"Idiots," Marina said as the girls backed away from the crate.

"I got poppers!" Manny said happily.

"Check it out! Sparklers!" Paul announced.

"All I see is snakes," I said a little disappointed.

"Grab them all, I'm sure we can figure out a way to use them to our advantage and if not, at least we can play with them afterwards," Eddie said through his mouth hole.

Manny reached in once more and pulled out something that looked shiny.

I thought maybe it was a scarf or something.

"What is it?" Marina asked.

Manny unraveled it and held it up for us all to see.

"Gross!" Paul yelled and covered his eyes.

"My eyes, my eyes!" I screamed.

A chorus of "eewws" and "yucks" came from the girls.

Eddie yelled, "GRANNY PANTIES!"

That was it! Manny threw them across the shed and all I could do was double over in laughter. Eddie was beside me on the floor holding his stomach from laughing so hard. Paul had tears of laughter in his eyes and the girls were standing together giggling in a huddle. Only Manny wasn't laughing. He was frantically trying to find someplace to wash the cooties from his hands. He was yelling, "Cooties, cooties, grandma cooties!"

"Who leaves underwear at the zoo?" Eddie said between bouts of laughter.

"I don't know? That's so weird," I agreed.

"Maybe it was a DARE! An old lady dare!" Eddie offered.

"An underwear dare? No way!" *I couldn't believe it, but what else could it be?*

Poor Manny. He was still trying to get rid of the cooties from touching the ginormous underwear. He tried wiping them on Paul, but Paul moved away too fast. He was heading toward me and I hid behind Eddie. Not the most honorable thing to do. Finally, Marina pointed to a canvas tent that was propped up against the shed wall.

"Use that," she said.

Manny practically leapt toward the tent and started wiping his hands down it.

"I don't think that is the best way to get rid of cooties," Bria said.

Manny turned around with a look of disbelief all over his face. "Then how?"

Chelsea bravely stepped up next to him and grabbed his forearm. She drew an imaginary circle on his arm while saying, "Circle, circle, dot, dot, now you have the cooties shot." She gave him a shot with an imaginary needle.

"No, that's not it." Bria took Manny's other arm and said, "Circle, circle, stir, stir, now you have the cooties cure." Bria used her finger to stir the cooties off him.

"No, no, move away. This is the real way to get rid of cooties." Marina pushed Chelsea and Bria away and began rubbing Manny's arm. Then she recited, "Circle, circle, fire, fire, now your cooties will expire."

Paul joined in on the cootie exorcism. He walked up to Manny and gave him a healthy punch in the shoulder. Manny stumbled back a bit. "Punch, punch, smack, smack, now the cooties can't come back."

"Um, thanks, I think." Manny rubbed his shoulder.

Now, I couldn't resist. "Circle, circle, spray, spray…"

Eddie interrupted my cooties cure because he had gotten some kind of long pipe from the corner and was holding it high. It had the granny panties hanging off the end. He was swinging it back and forth like a mad man. "Circle, circle, square, square, now the cooties are everywhere!"

The shed wasn't that big but that didn't stop us from running around like crazy, trying to evade the panties. I guess there was a little bit of bully left in Eddie.

"Enough, Eddie. Stop!" Marina said in a very stern voice, just like when a teacher has reached the end of her rope.

Surprisingly, he stopped. He really must have a crush on her; otherwise, he would have kept going until someone got upset. Usually me.

"Sorry, everyone. I was trying to lighten up the mood." He flung the granny panties and they went sailing. They landed above a picture of a much younger Hog that said, *Employee of the Month, July, 1998.* Bulls-eye!

We all sighed with relief; we knew that was a close call with the cooties. Rumor has it if you get the cooties, you must quarantine yourself for at least a week and you have to take a shower with orange juice. And it has to be the really pulpy kind.

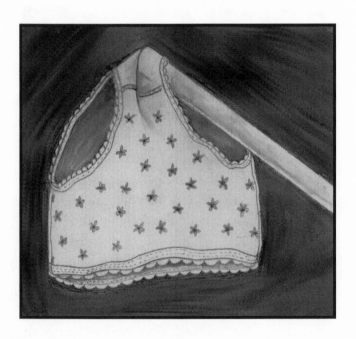

Granny Panties

CHAPTER 16

Eddie had some trouble getting the golf cart out of the shed. It lunged forward, then he braked hard and jerked it forward again. In the process, he knocked over two canisters, three boxes and just about ran over Chelsea's foot. She barely got out of the way in the nick of time.

We closed the shed doors as Eddie worked on trying to maneuver the golf cart.

"Okay, guys. I think I got the hang of this now. Hop on!" he said.

Marina, Chelsea and Bria hopped into the backseat and I scrambled in the front. Manny had his new skates on and Paul was riding the skateboard. We looked like the very opposite of an intimidating gang. We were more like a ragtag group of misfits. We had a big monkey driving the cart, me holding a sleeping baby monkey, the girls with petting zoo snacks and two boys acting like they were part of some extreme sports team. Paul had already fallen twice and Manny was holding onto the cart for support. At this point, I think the monkeys had a better chance of capturing us tonight.

"We should probably start at the Petting Zoo," Eddie said.

"Yeah, if I were a monkey, I would look there first," Marina said.

"Why?" I asked.

"It's obvious, Josh. If you were looking for a baby, that's where all the baby animals are," Eddie explained.

"That's right, Eddie," Marina agreed.

Eddie beamed. It was weird to hear them agree on something. We headed to the Petting Zoo.

"There, up in the tree!" Paul screamed and pointed.

We all looked up. There was a rustling in the tree and leaves were falling everywhere.

"That has to be one of them," Manny said.

It was. It looked like one of the females. She wasn't as big as the other ones. At least it wasn't the Colonel. I sighed with relief.

Eddie slammed on the breaks and the girls jumped off.

"Okay, let's do this!" Chelsea said.

Marina held on to her replacement walkie-talkie.

The three of them walked to the entrance of the Petting Zoo holding hands. They made a very formidable chain.

"Maybe we shouldn't leave them alone," I said.

"Naw, they will be all right. We have to find the other monkeys. They know the drill. I have confidence in them, don't you?"

I wasn't sure how to answer. We went over and over the relay plan, but what if something went awry? "No, I do. It's just that so many things could go wrong," I said.

"I was thinking the same thing. Maybe we need a designated lookout. I think it's going to have to be you, Josh," Eddie said.

"Yeah, that sounds good," Paul chimed in while trying to keep his balance on the skate-board.

"Yeah, Josh, be the lookout," Manny said.

"I can't, I have to be ahead of everyone with little Chortles here. Why can't you be the lookout, Eddie?"

"I have to blend in and watch from the inside. I am much better at fixing problems if

167

something goes wrong. You will have to be the lookout from the Canopy Café balcony," Eddie said.

I couldn't argue that point because Eddie was definitely better from the inside. I did like the idea of seeing what was going on with everyone. "Okay, I'll do it. But then the baby monkey exchange will have to happen after all the monkeys are back in the Primate Palace. Can we do that?"

Eddie's big monkey head nodded. Then he fumbled through his backpack and pulled out two headsets with microphones. He cut off one of the monkey ears. He placed a little earphone receiver in his ear and then placed the microphone transmitter around his head. He then handed me a headset. "Put it on."

"Say something into the headset, Josh," he ordered

I cleared my throat, "Um, testing 1, 2, 3."

Eddie touched his ear. "Perfect, I heard that perfectly, even though it was so very unoriginal. So now, you can keep me informed about what is going on every single second."

I was getting ready to say something snarky when we heard some hoots and hollers in the distance.

"Quickly, to Big Cat Country!" Paul said and sped off with Manny following.

"Josh, let's get you back to the Tree House so you can start picket duty."

"What?" I asked.

"Picket duty. It is a military term. It's also known as the lookout. Didn't you read the list of military terms I left for you on your desk last month? I put a lot of time and energy into making that for you," Eddie said.

"Are you kidding me? That got you in a lot of trouble. You didn't finish your homework, but had time to make a military list. You got grounded, remember?"

"Yeah, I know. I wasn't allowed to watch the Military Channel for two whole days. That was one of the tougher punishments I've had this year," he laughed.

I looked at him dumbfounded.

"I know that look, Josh. Are you backing out? This is just like the time you caused us to get grounded for two weeks," Eddie said.

"What? That was because of you, not me. Drawing eyebrows on Alwilda was your idea!"

"I just wanted her to look surprised when I walked in the room. What's wrong with that? It was hilarious. And I learned an important lesson: Sharpie markers don't wash off. I wish we could have gotten a picture of it before we got busted."

"We? All I did was walk in the same time as Dad. I had nothing to do with it."

"I know. But when you started laughing, Jack just assumed you were part of it," Eddie said.

"I couldn't help it. Alwilda looked hilarious. You really did a good job on her eyebrows. She did look surprised. But did you have to give her a twirly mustache, too?" I said.

"Everyone knows twirly mustaches are the funniest of all mustaches."

A big smile spread across my face. as I remembered that day. "But still, I shouldn't have gotten grounded." I stopped smiling.

"No, you're right. But that was the only time this year that I got you into trouble." Eddie said as he veered the golf cart in the direction of the tree house.

"Really, do you want me to name them all? I'm keeping track. How about when we shook talcum powder all over our room so it would look like it was snowing? Or how about when you poured rubber cement on the stairs so I would get stuck? Or how about the time you dented Allie's car because you fell out of the tree. And then the latest was the bubblegum explosion on the bus. Want me to go on?" I asked.

"First of all, I hardly had to talk you into the talcum powder thing. You wanted it to snow as bad as I did. It was like over a hundred degrees outside that day. Who knew that breathing talcum powder was bad for you? And the only reason I put rubber cement on the stairs was because the advertisement said *money back guarantee* if it didn't work, and I had run out of allowance. I didn't think it would actually work. And falling out of the tree was your fault. We were playing hide and seek. Who knew we had such weak trees? You would have never found me had I not fallen." Eddie said and hit the brakes. He dropped me off for my picket duty, gave me a serious salute, and then sped away.

CHAPTER 17

I nervously paced back and forth on the Canopy Café balcony. I scanned the zoo using the night vision binoculars. My stomach was in knots. How could I let my friends talk me into this? I didn't want to admit it, but I was scared being alone.

Chortles whined like he was scared too, so I tried to think of something to soothe him. Got it! I remembered how my dad would sing to me when I was little if I was scared of something.

I started singing my dad's song about a little lost bunny. It didn't work until I got to the part where the little bunny sings. I made my voice really high, like my dad used to. Bingo! It worked. Chortles settled back down.

I kept singing in the high, bunny voice and I added some bunny movements, too.

Suddenly, an extended flash of light lit up the night! It was like a strobe and it lasted forever. I didn't want Chortles to freak out so I kept singing, even though I was temporarily blinded. Finally, it stopped and I rubbed my eyes. I thought I heard some rustling in the trees above my head.

"What is going on up there?" Eddie asked through the two way headset.

"I'm blind!"

"What? How?"

"A big flash of light, while I was looking through the night vision binoculars."

"I'm on my way! Just stay put! Give your wimpy eyes time to adjust!"

While I waited for Eddie, I kept thinking about that flash. It seemed to go on forever. What could have made it? I could only think of one thing...but that was impossible.

A few minutes later, Eddie ran up to me huffing and puffing.

"How many fingers am I holding up?" he asked as he waved two fingers and his thumb inches away from my face.

"Two," I answered.

"Noooooo! You're blind! I was holding up three! It's all my fault. I knew you weren't ready for picket duty alone."

"Calm down, Eddie. You were holding up two fingers….and a thumb."

"Very funny, Josh."

"Gotcha!"

Just then, Marina called over the walkie-talkie. "We've got some action here!" she said.

I looked through the binoculars, my eyesight having returned, and I couldn't believe what I saw!

"What do you see?" Eddie asked.

"Amazing! Marina is riding the donkey, Bria is riding the pony, and Chelsea is riding the alpaca."

"That's hardly amazing."

"And one of the monkeys is riding a goat!"

"Yes! That is awesome!" Eddie said.

"Now the girls are trying hard to corral the monkey on the goat, like cowgirls going after a stray calf! Look at them go! The goat is trying to buck off the monkey, but the monkey is holding fast."

I watched in amazement as the little monkey rode the goat like a bull rider going for a whirlwind ride. The goat bucked and kicked, but the little monkey hung on; with one monkey paw gripping the goat's horns on the top of its head and the other paw flailing wildly in the air.

Eddie grabbed the binoculars from me to get a look, "That's the coolest thing I've ever seen!"

I grabbed the binoculars from him and he grabbed them back from me. We got in a tussle back and forth to see who would get them. Neither of us wanted to miss a thing. We ended up sharing the binoculars with one eye each peering through.

I watched as another monkey opened the Petting Zoo gate. The monkey riding the goat ran out. This was way better than any movie I'd ever seen. I watched in astonishment as all the goats ran out of the Petting Zoo.

I heard Eddie say, "My plan is working perfectly!"

"You planned to set the goats free?"

"No, I planned for the girls to lead some of the monkeys to the Primate Palace."

"And…"

"And, it's working."

Eddie was right. My crazy step-brother was right. I watched the second monkey jump on another goat while the girls road their steeds in hot pursuit. That monkey was holding on to the goat's horns like it was steering a car. It was a sight to see. When the monkey pulled the horns to the left, the goat turned to the left; when the monkey pulled the horns to the right, the goat turned to the right. These monkeys were smarter than we thought. The girls were riding their steeds, right behind the monkeys. They were steering them straight for Big Cat Country.

"Woo-hoo!" Marina called over the walkie-talkie. "We're bringing them in!"

"Great job, girls!" I answered. "Keep going all the way around!"

"Will do, Josh!" she answered breathlessly. I could tell she was having the time of her life.

Just then, we got a call from Manny.

"Help! Help! They're after us! The bananas worked too good!" he said as he huffed and puffed.

Eddie grabbed the walkie-talkie and shoved the binoculars at me, "Calm down! Tell me exactly what's going on!"

"I lost Paul! He fell off the skateboard. He is a terrible skateboard rider! I tried to tell him so after the fifth time he fell, but he wouldn't listen to me. It's bad. So very bad. The monkeys ate all the bananas! They came after us for more, but we were all out…we were all out!" he wailed.

"Listen, Manny; you can do this! You're the fastest boy in school. You're even faster now that you're skating. Are you listening? I have a plan to save Paul."

"Okay," he said softly.

"I see him! Manny is by the kayaks." I said, and then I scanned Big Cat Country for Paul. "I found Paul. Not good. Two monkeys have him cornered up against a railing just a few feet away from the lion's cage. Eddie, you'd better put your plan into action quick, before that lion decides to make his move."

"Right," he said, and turned his attention to the problem at hand. "Manny, you've gotta skate like the wind. You must go back to Big Cat Country and grab a bunch of plantains on the way. Don't stop! You'll have to grab them as you skate by. Go now! You can do it!"

I watched Manny make an about face. He took off like a rocket. I've never seen anyone move so fast! He was back in Big Cat Country in seconds. I watched him pluck the plantains as he skated by. Perfect!

"Josh, tell me when he's there," Eddie said.

"Will do," I answered. Eddie and I were working like a well-oiled machine.

I watched the monkeys approach Paul and then they stopped. My gut sank as I watched them reach behind their bottoms. They were getting ready to launch their greatest weapon: Poop!

Then, the poop began to fly. It was like the Aviary all over again. Paul hid behind the skateboard. At least he had some control over it when he used it like a shield. He began furiously swatting the poop with it. The poop rebounded and stuck to the lion's mane. We heard the lion's angry roar all the way from the balcony.

Just then, Manny arrived with the plantains.

"He's there!" I said to Eddie.

Eddie pressed the walkie-talkie button and yelled to Manny, "Release the plantains!"

Manny showered the manic monkeys with plantains, which they greedily ate. Just then, the girls arrived on their steeds, whooping and hollering at the monkeys riding the goats just ahead of them. As soon as the other monkeys saw the plantains, they leapt off the goats and started chowing down, too. I saw Paul jump on the donkey with Marina and they took off.

The monkeys quickly gobbled their treats and took off after my friends. Somehow the hunters had become the hunted. I knew this wouldn't end well.

"Um, Eddie?"

"Yeah?"

"They're moving pretty fast through the zoo."

"Yep."

"How are we going to get to the Primate Palace before them?"

"I think you already know."

Eddie was right. I already knew. We looked at each other and nodded. Then we sprinted to the zip-line platform which led to Alligator Alley.

My girlie screams could be heard all over the zoo. They even scared little Chortles. He burrowed deeper into my backpack. I don't know why, but I decided this was a great time to have a conversation about the safety of the zip-line with Eddie. I was pretty sure Hog said it wasn't ready for use, but I couldn't quite remember. I yelled to Eddie, but it was really hard to hear with the wind whipping around our heads.

"Hey Eddie!" I yelled, "Remember when Hog said this zip-line wasn't ready for use?" I screamed.

"What? You are going to land on your caboose?"

"No! I thought Hog said that they had a few accidents on this zip-line!"

"You had an accident? Then you definitely should not land on your caboose! That's just gross!" he yelled back.

I was about ready to yell that I had not had an accident, but I was too terrified. Then I noticed what was coming next; directly below my feet swam fifty of the biggest alligators I'd ever seen. They saw me approach and began jumping out of the water. One even missed my toes by inches! I heard their jaws snapping as they tried to make me their late night snack. Their reptilian eyes glowed menacingly in the moonlight. I tucked my feet close to my body just in time to prevent the biggest one from snapping my legs clean off! And all the while that weird strobe light was flashing, just like before. I felt like I was in a horror movie.

Finally, after what seemed like a twenty minute zip over teeth and tails, I landed on the other side, squarely on my bottom. Eddie had landed before me and was laughing so hard that no sound came out and he was literally crying.

"You! You!" he stammered, struggling to get the words out, gasping for breath through his laughter.

I dusted myself off. "What's so funny?"

"You, you, you," he took a very deep breath, "You said you had a poop accident, and landed…" He couldn't finish because he was doubled over with laughter. Finally he got it out, "You landed on your butt!"

"I did not!"

"Yes, you did! I watched you. I also heard your girlie screams."

"Fine! I'll admit my screams were girlie, but that's only because a giant alligator almost bit off my leg."

"A giant alligator?"

"Yes."

"Did you read the zoo brochure?"

"No."

"City Zoo has twenty baby alligators that currently live in Alligator Alley. The largest one is two feet long."

"That can't be right..." I trailed off.

"It is, but there's no time to debate that now. Pull up your poop pants and let's capture some us some monkeys." Eddie took off running through the zoo.

I tugged on my pants. They had slipped down a bit, but they were not full of poop! I sprinted after Eddie with Chortles bouncing around in my backpack.

CHAPTER 18

Eddie fumbled with the master key. "I almost got it," he said, as he attempted to unlock the old Primate Palace. "Now here's how it's gonna play out. I'll run through the palace and unlock the back gate. You stay here and wait for our friends to ride through. Then, at the last minute, after the monkeys enter, you set Chortles down and hightail it outta here. Got it?"

"Yeah," I said weakly.

Eddie opened the gate and we walked inside. It was actually an outdoor area, kinda like an arena but with little side doors leading to covered rooms in case of bad weather. The outside part was surrounded by an old moat and a fence. I knew the monkeys would be safe here. I scooped little Chortles out of my back pack and he clung on to me for dear life. I guess the night's escapades had frightened him. He was shaking a little. I petted him and that calmed him down a bit.

I followed Eddie to the back gate. He unlocked it and stood, blocking the exit.

"Okay Josh, it's time to man up. Go back to the front gate and wait for our friends. They'll be here any minute. Let them go right by you so they can exit quickly. If you have any trouble or get into a tight spot with the Colonel, use your secret weapon." He shoved me forward.

I reluctantly walked back to the entrance. I decided to give myself a pep talk on the way. *I can do this. If I get stuck, I'll use my secret weapon. Yeah, that will work. Wait. I don't have a secret weapon, do I?*

"Hey Eddie," I called from across the compound, "What's my secret weapon?"

"Same as theirs!" he yelled back.

"Same as who's?"

"The monkeys!"

"What's their secret weapon?" I screamed, getting more nervous by the minute.

"If they attack, just throw your poop. You have plenty after that zip-line!"

I swear I heard him laughing across the compound. I was getting ready to defend myself again when I saw a sight by the moonlight that made my blood turn cold.

My friends were moving at full speed and they were headed straight towards me. From high atop the trees, the monkeys pursued with bared teeth and warrior cries.

Marina, Paul, and the donkey flew through the gate first. I barely had time to step to the side.

"They're coming!" Marina yelled.

"Save yourself!" Paul added as they rode to safety.

Bria was next on the pony. "So angry! The monkeys are so angry! Take cover!" And she too was gone in a flash.

"Dude, run!" Manny said, as he zipped by on his skates.

Chelsea was next on her alpaca, "Jump on, Josh!" she said, as she brought the animal to a halt.

I swooned. She was the only one who tried to rescue me. But I couldn't let her get hurt. Plus, I had a job to do. Eddie was right, it was time for me to man up. I hit the alpaca on the rump and it shot off like an arrow, carrying her to safety. And then the monkeys were upon me.

They leapt from the trees and sprinted full force to where I was standing. Two young males and two females. They formed a semi-circle right in front of me. Razor sharp teeth glistened in the moonlight. They were watching me and waiting. But what for? Somehow I already knew.

I watched the semi-circle of monkeys part as. the Colonel strolled through the opening. He stopped three feet from me and bared his teeth and screamed.

Something inside me snapped. I had had enough! Enough poop flung at me, enough wild monkeys screaming at me, enough crazy antics through the zoo and enough of being scared. I opened my mouth and I screamed loud and long right back at him. And then something weird happened.

The Colonel cocked his head to one side and stretched his arms out to me. I realized he wanted Chortles. I tried to pry Chortles from my neck, but his little monkey paws were really strong. He wouldn't budge.

The Colonel took a few steps closer. I sang softly into Chortles ear. I sang the little bunny song. He relaxed enough to let go. I mustered up all my courage and handed him to the Colonel. The Colonel sniffed him and petted him. He handed him to his mom, who cradled him protectively in her arms.

Then something incredible happened that I never thought I'd see: the Colonel saluted me. He actually saluted me. I didn't know what to do, so I saluted him back. I saw respect in his eyes.

I started to turn to walk out the back gate, no longer afraid. But before I did, I saw Eddie gingerly lock the front gate. He must have run back to the front after opening the back gate. Good thinking.

I walked through the Primate Palace and closed the back gate. Eddie huffed and puffed as he met me there. He locked this gate too, but it was not necessary. The monkeys didn't even try to follow me out. I think they were too tired from the night's adventures. They just curled up together under a tree and fell asleep. That actually sounded like a good plan to me.

CHAPTER 19

We were in the gift shop, returning the items we had borrowed to complete our big monkey rescue. Eddie insisted we put everything back in order before we called it a night. He said it was our duty as Junior Zookeepers to keep all parts of the zoo in tip top shape, even the gift shop.

Eddie sat in the corner, trying to restuff the big stuffed monkey by the light of a key ring flash light.

"Almost done. No one will ever be able to tell I used it for the best and most exciting adventure of my life."

Just then, the lights turned on and we all cheered.

I looked at Eddie and the stuffed monkey and burst out laughing. Not only did it look misshapen but it was missing a nose, an ear, two eyes, and a mouth.

"Eddie, I'm afraid you'll have to purchase this one. No one is going to buy it that way."

"You might be right, Josh."

"It was a hundred dollars," I said.

"Yeah, I know." He looked sad.

Just then Hog staggered in. He looked like he had seen better days. "What's going on? How'd you all get in here? Wait, are those my keys?" He was looking right at Eddie.

"Yes, sir," Eddie said meekly as he handed the keys over to Hog. Busted.

Hog grabbed the keys and went to hang them on his belt, when he noticed they were sticky. He inspected them closer, honing in on the key that had some gum on the tip. He scraped it off with his fingernail and tasted it. "Grape?"

"Ah, sort of," Eddie answered.

"Seems like you kids have a story you need to tell."

Eddie wasted no time reconstructing the events of the night. Even though I was there, I sat enthralled as he retold our tale. I noticed Hog was squirming by the time Eddie reached the end.

"That's some adventure," Hog said and scratched his head. "It seems to me like I owe you kids a big thanks. And if we could keep this just between us, well, then I probably won't lose my job. Yep, I really do love it here…" he trailed off with teary eyes.

Eddie looked crestfallen. "You mean we can't tell anyone ever?"

"You could, but I'd be unemployed as soon as they found out I shot myself in the butt with a tranquilizer dart again."

"Again? Exactly how many times has it happened?" I asked dumbfounded.

"Let's see…there was the time when I was trying to tranquilize the big male lion for his dental work. Then, there was the time when I was cleaning the dart gun, and before that, um…" He thought for a minute. "Yeah, there was also another dart gun cleaning accident. So I guess three?"

"All in the butt? But how?" Marina asked.

"That is a story for another time. The sun will be up soon and the other workers will be arriving. So we need to finish getting the gift shop in order," he said and I could tell he was embarrassed because he turned bright red. I guess we had that in common.

"So do we have a deal?" he asked us.

"Deal," I said right away. I figured I could keep a secret longer than Hog could keep a job. Eventually, I would get to tell the story.

Everyone else agreed quickly, but Eddie. He looked miserable.

"Come on, Eddie," I said. "All the really cool people already know the story because they were here with us living it."

"Alright. I'll keep your secret, Mr. Hog," Eddie said and held out his hand for Hog to shake.

Instead of shaking his hand, Hog put a gift card in it. "I got this when I was employee of the month. That was a while ago as you can imagine. I never used it, but I think it should cover the price of that big stuffed monkey, plus a few more souvenirs for the rest of you guys."

Eddie grinned from ear to ear. The girls hugged Hog. His face got red all over again but you could tell he was happy. We left our souvenirs piled high on the gift shop counter so we could pay for them later with the gift card. I wanted my safari hat with the flash light attached. So did Paul and Manny. Marina wanted the stuffed Chortles and Paul gave his stuffed Chortles to Bria. Not to be left out, Chelsea grabbed a stuffed Chortles too. Eddie was very content to have the gigantic monkey. Everything else that we used we put back.

"Okay, I gotta go check on those monkeys. I guess the old Primate Palace is going to be their home for a while until we get that tree removed. Do I need to round up the Petting Zoo animals, too?" Hog asked us.

"We got the pony, donkey, and alpaca back in the Petting Zoo." Marina said proudly.

"I'm impressed girls, that alpaca is a handful. You kids really are Junior Zookeepers!" Hog said.

"We take the job very seriously," Eddie said proudly.

"Why, I guess you do. You are the first group of students I have ever seen here in my twenty years that actually had an honest-to-goodness, real life, genuine, zoo experience," Hog announced.

"Yeah, but we still couldn't find the goats," Chelsea added.

"We looked everywhere," Bria said.

"I hope they're alright," Marina said with concern.

"Don't worry about those silly goats, they get loose quite often and I always find them in the same place," He said.

"Where is that?" I asked.

"There is an area out back that's chockfull of roses and honeysuckle vines. They love to eat that stuff. I always find them there."

"I would think they would eat the grassy areas," I said.

"Very common misconception, Josh. You are thinking of sheep. Goats like trees and bushes, but sheep love to graze on grass, right Mr. Hog?" Eddie added.

"You are right, son. Goats are known to be scavengers. If you let them, they will eat just about anything first before grass. Well, I've even seen them eat ice cream cones that kids have dropped, tennis shoes, and heck, they will even nibble on your clothes. How do you know so much about goats?" He asked Eddie.

We all sighed knowing Eddie was ready to launch into a goat lecture. I had to do something fast.

"Uh, Hog. I think I can hear the monkeys," I said.

"Right, let me go check on them. You kids go back to the tree house and get to bed. I will see you all at breakfast. I make a mean hash brown scramble. I'm kinda known for it," he bragged.

"Sounds good. What's a scramble?" Eddie asked.

"What I do is start with hash browns in a little bit of butter and then I add some…," Hog said.

I interrupted him, "Hog, the monkeys!"

"Oh, right, yes. I'm on my way." He started walking to the old Primate Palace.

"Geez, Josh. I really wanted to hear how he makes the scramble," Eddie said.

I looked around at my friends; I could see how tired everyone was. "Come on guys, let's go back to the tree house and go to bed," I suggested. "It's been a long night." Everyone nodded in agreement.

As we climbed the stairs, Eddie began his lecture. "So as I was going to say, I watched this program called, *Petting Zoos and the Animals that Live in Them*, and was fascinated by the goats. For instance, did you know that a goat's pupils are rectangular?" Eddie was talking to no one in particular.

"Really?" I couldn't help it, because it was interesting.

"That's really weird," Paul said.

"Yep, it sure is. The only other animal with rectangular pupils is the octopus. Yep. It gives them both excellent night vision," Eddie said.

"What else did you learn?" Manny asked.

Eddie continued, "There are at least two hundred different breeds of goats. Some are called fainting goats. When they get scared, they faint."

"No way!" I said.

"Oh yeah, they freeze for about five or ten seconds and then fall over on their side. It is hilarious," Eddie explained.

"I don't think that is funny, I think it's sad," Marina said.

"It doesn't hurt them at all. It's just their defense," Eddie said softly.

"Do you know anything else about them that isn't sad?" Chelsea asked.

Girls can be so weird. Personally, I thought it was hilarious.

"It has been said that people eat goat meat and drink goat milk more than any other animal in the world," Eddie offered.

"More than cows?" Bria asked.

"Yeah."

"That's interesting, but I think I'll become a vegetarian anyway," Marina said.

Eddie smiled. "Not me, ever."

CHAPTER 20

My head hit the soft, fluffy pillow and I was asleep instantly. I dreamt of crazy monkeys, zip-lines, exploding gum and strawberry cake. I could have slept the whole day away, but a terrible screeching sound woke me from my slumber. At first I thought it was a Treefoot, and then I realized it was just Freiberger.

"What are you boys doing still asleep? The sun's been up for over an hour already," she squawked.

Eddie burrowed deeper into his sleeping bag. "Eddie need sleepy," he groaned.

"You have exactly fifteen minutes to meet me at the Canopy Café for a hearty breakfast. Your parents will be here shortly to pick you up." Her shoes heels clicked noisily across the wooden floor as she exited the room.

What a drill sergeant.

"Come on, guys," Manny said. "I'm ready for some of Hog's hash brown scramble."

That did it. Eddie literally jumped out of his sleeping bag and into his pants, shirt, and shoes without missing a beat. We all followed suit and headed upstairs behind him. The girls were already there.

In the center of the table was a gigantic platter like the kind you see at Thanksgiving with a turkey on it. Instead of a turkey, it was piled high with Hog's very own hash brown scramble.

"Morning boys, I was just telling the girls all the ingredients in my hash brown scramble. See, I used every delicious breakfast food that kids love to eat. I'll start at the bottom."

As he said this, he pulled a pointer out of his back pants pocket and waved it around the bottom of his creation. "If you look closely, you'll find pancakes and waffles make up the base, layered of course, for extra strength. The butter and syrup act like glue if you will. The middle is covered with a combination of hash browns mixed with scrambled eggs, sausage and bacon. Delish. I suggest a little ketchup when you reach this layer," he said proudly.

I looked at Eddie. The poor guy, he was practically salivating.

"The top is full of mini-donuts. You can pluck them off and dip them in milk. But here's the real ingenious part: I topped each donut with little Cheerios cereal pressed on them. You gotta have some oats for breakfast. Am I right?" he asked.

"See, Eddie," I said, "Like I said before, Cheerios are made of oats." That's when I noticed Eddie was tearing up.

"It's beautiful! The ultimate breakfast!" he cried. And it really was.

"Mr. Hog, you should be a chef!" Eddie said and we all cheered.

Hog swelled up with pride. Maybe he had finally found his calling.

Somehow we were all famished, even though we had snacked all night long. Eddie said that you burn double the calories when you're on an adventure and I'm pretty sure he was right.

Freiberger couldn't help but lecture us as we ate. "I know that Mr. Hog did a good job watching after you kids while I was, well, indisposed, but I can't help but think you all wasted an opportunity."

We all looked at each other but kept our mouths closed, except for Eddie.

"What opportunity?" he asked.

I was actually thinking the same thing and by the expressions on their faces, I knew they were thinking it, too.

"The golden opportunity to witness the zoo at night and to see the nocturnal behavior of the animals. Mr. Hog told me you were all in bed by 7:00 pm. I'm a little disappointed. I guess it's more important to sit around and play on your phones and laptops, or whatever it is you play on, than to experience nature. You might have been able to interact with real animals; supervised by Mr. Hog, of course."

Not wanting to get Hog into any trouble we all stayed silent except for Eddie. Surprise, surprise.

"We couldn't play on our phones because they fell in the water. Don't you remember?" Eddie reminded her.

I shot Eddie a look that was meant to stop him from talking. He got the hint.

"My goodness, I forgot about that. I will explain to your parents. Well, did it ever occur to you to learn something about each other you didn't know or maybe come together as a team to figure out a solution to a problem one of you had? This was supposed to be a learning experience."

If only Freiberger knew the truth! There was no way our adventure could have been successful if we hadn't all worked together as a team.

Eddie raised his hand again.

"Yes, Edward?" Freiberger said.

"I learned that Manny's nana taught him how to make him plantains."

Manny smiled and spoke up. "I learned that Marina wants to become a vegetarian."

Marina pushed her plate away. "Yes I do, starting tomorrow. Breakfast was too good. I learned that Paul knows how to skateboard, sort of."

"I learned that Bria knows how to ride a pony," Paul offered.

Bria giggled a bit. "I learned that Chelsea likes Honey Smacks cereal."

"I learned that Josh used to sing the song, Big Rock Candy Mountain with his grandpa," Chelsea added.

"I love that song,!" Ms. Freiberger said excitedly.

Apparently, Freiberger didn't remember singing that song while we threw pills down her throat because of the bee stings. She was pretty out of it.

Freiberger looked at me. I was the only one who hadn't spoken up yet. What did I learn? I actually learned a lot. I learned that any mission could be accomplished by team-work, cooperation, and respect. I also learned I had an amazing step-brother and friends I would do anything for and who would do anything for me.

"Well, Josh. Did you learn anything?" Ms. Freiberger asked.

I cleared my throat and said, "I learned the legend of the Treefoot from Eddie!"

The entire table started laughing except for Freiberger.

"There is no such thing, Edward. Stop making up these…" Ms, Freiberger stopped mid-sentence because Hog walked in carrying our cellphone bag.

"Look what I found!" Hog exclaimed.

"Our phones!" Bria squealed.

We made a beeline for Hog. We couldn't wait to get our phones back in our hands. Funny thing is, as soon as we got them, we tossed them into our backpacks and sat back at the breakfast table and continued talking.

"There's another thing I forgot to tell you guys about the Treefoot," Eddie said and we all leaned in to hear.

"They have small leaves that sprout from their branch-like feet. And they change color with the seasons, just like real leaves."

"Absolute nonsense," Ms. Freiberger said.

"You mean they can turn red and gold?" Manny asked.

"Yup."

Just then, Hog got a call saying that our parents were waiting at the entrance of the zoo to pick us up. We all made our way back down to our rooms to pick up our bags. I took one final look at Alligator Alley from the window. I couldn't believe that I'd zip-lined over it. It all seemed like a fuzzy dream now. It was real, but I didn't have any proof except for my memory. We paid for our souvenirs with Hog's gift card and walked to the zoo's entrance.

We said goodbye to our friends. No long drawn out goodbyes. Heck, we'd see them on Monday. Still, when we parted, you could tell we were all a little bit closer. Kinda like a troop or a team. I had this weird feeling we'd have a lot more adventures in our future.

I walked to my car with a big smile on my face.

CHAPTER 21

Being back at the house was kind of a letdown. I could tell Eddie felt the same way. I watched Eddie tip-toe into Alwilda's room carrying the gigantic stuffed monkey. He tip-toed back out again. Even though Eddie had huge caveman feet, he was surprisingly quiet around Alwilda when she napped.

"I hope she likes it," Eddie said to me.

"I dunno, Eddie. It is pretty big. Maybe you shouldn't leave it in there for when she wakes up. She might be scared of it. Maybe you should introduce it to her, like it is your friend," I suggested.

Eddie thought for a moment. "Yeah, you may be right about that, Josh. The last thing I want to do is scare her. She's so little," he said.

"Yeah, but not as little as baby Chortles," I said. Wow, I missed him.

"Yeah, he thought you were his mother." Eddie laughed and tip-toed back in her room to get the monkey.

I should have gotten mad at that last comment, but I didn't mind because Chortles did like me and I had grown fond of him. I think I might ask for a zoo pass for my birthday so I could watch him grow up. I headed upstairs to work on my homework.

I was sitting at my desk when I felt a furry hand on my left shoulder. "Nice try, Eddie. I know it's you."

Eddie said in a low, growly voice, "It's not Eddie, it's the Colonel and I want Chortles NOW!" Eddie doubled over laughing, throwing the big monkey on his bed.

I looked at the monkey. "Are you going to be a monkey next fall for Halloween? You already have a great costume," I said.

"Nope. I think I'm going to be Treefoot instead," he said.

I wish I thought of that! "That would be awesome. Hey, do you know how to make a Treefoot costume?" I asked.

"Naw, but it shouldn't be too hard. I should probably get started, seeing how there is only seven months to go until Halloween. There has to be a video on it. I'll just search 'trees + monkeys,' that should pull something up." Eddie sat down on his bean bag chair and opened his laptop.

I knew once Eddie got on his computer to play, his homework would never get done. I went back to working on mine.

After a few moments, I heard a terrible scream, like a girl who was very frightened. What was Eddie watching? I looked at him and noticed he was laughing really hard, his signature laugh—no sound coming out, tears streaming down his face and his shoulders were shaking.

"Josh," he gasped for breath. "It's…the… best…thing, EVER!" He gasped again. "I, I, I can't stop laughing…too funny!"

He took a couple of deep breaths and said, "Monkeys, and trees and YOU!" And he started cry-laughing again.

Me? I stood behind him to see what was so funny. There I was, on the laptop screen, zip-lining down Alligator Alley, screaming my head off like a little girl. But how?

There was only one possible solution. The monkeys did it! Somehow they videotaped me with my own phone and then hit an instant upload to the internet. That explained that weird flashing light I saw when I was zip-lining. It was the video flash! Those monkeys were really tech savvy.

Eddie hit the replay button and started laughing all over again. Then he shoved the laptop at me. "That's so funny, I gotta pee," he said and ran to the bathroom.

My stomach did a flip-flop when I noticed it already had one million hits. Oh no! It had gone viral! I was shocked. My life was definitely over. But wait, no one could really see my face. I was saved! Only my true friends knew it was me and they wouldn't tell because we promised to keep our adventure a secret. Thank goodness.

Eddie strolled back in and plopped into the bean bag chair. I handed him his laptop and sat in a bean bag chair right next to him.

"That was the best video I have ever seen in my life!" He tapped on the keyboard. "I just shared it with all our friends."

"Thanks a lot," I said sarcastically.

"Sorry Josh, you have to share that quality of work with the world."

"I guess. It's weird though, that the monkeys were able to figure out how to do that."

"Not at all. It makes perfect sense. Haven't you heard the expression, *monkey see, monkey do?*" he asked.

"Ah, yeah. Everyone's heard it. So what?"

"So, those monkeys spend their whole day watching people take videos of them. It just makes sense that they want to take a few videos of us."

Eddie's explanation actually did make some sense. Still, something didn't seem right. Just then I remembered something awful. That weird flashing light also happened when I was singing the little bunny song to Chortles.

"Um, Eddie. Can you do a search and see if there's a video of me singing the little bunny song to Chortles?"

Eddie typed in "boy + singing + bunny + monkey," and got a hit. He handed me the laptop and looked over my shoulder.

There I was singing in a high pitched voice and hopping around like a fool. It was worse than I ever could have imagined: two million hits and my face was very clear!

Eddie was literally rolling on the floor and gasping for breath.

My face turned bright red, but not from embarrassment, but from anger. I had just figured something out and Eddie was about to feel my wrath. "Eddie!" I yelled. "I know it was you!"

He stopped laughing for a moment and looked surprised. "What?" Then he started laughing again. "Okay, you got me. I uploaded them earlier. I found them on your phone when I was recharging both our phones. Your welcome. By the way, it was super hard not to tell you right away, but I wanted it to go viral. I was laughing so hard the first time I watched it I accidently farted. I farted so hard that a little bit of poop came out. I had to throw my underwear in the laundry instantly. But I promise the monkeys really did take the videos. By the way, how'd you figure it out?"

"Let's see. One, I noticed that they are uploaded by someone with the screen name: Sir Edward Fartsickle of Burpytown. That could only be you. And two, the videos are labeled. Let's see, the first one is labeled, *My Brother Screams Like a Girl*. Real original. And the second one is labeled, *My Brother Sings and Dances Like a Girl*. Well at least you had a theme. Oh, by the way, YOU'RE DEAD!"

Then I executed a world class ninja move. In one swift motion, I set down the laptop, leapt out of the beanbag chair and pounced on Eddie with all my might while screaming a terrifying, "HI-YA!"

We rolled on the floor wrestling. I was actually getting the best of Eddie. He wasn't fighting up to his potential because he was laughing again. It was frustrating.

Through his laughter he kept saying over and over again, "It was worth it! It was so worth it! And your ninja 'HI-YA' sounded like a girl!"

Just then my dad and Allie came into the room.

"What's going on?" my dad asked.

We immediately separated. "Nothing," we both muttered simultaneously.

"We were just fooling around, ninja style." Eddie said.

"Is that true, Josh?" Allie asked.

"Yep." I answered. I figured I'd save my revenge for another time.

"Well, good because we have a surprise for both of you," she beamed.

Eddie beat me to the punch, "What is it?" He quickly slammed down the top of the laptop so they wouldn't see what was on the screen. Or who was on it!

Allie handed us a stack of brochures. "We were very impressed with you two during the zoo field trip. We didn't get any calls from the chaperones. We didn't even get any calls from the two of you."

"That's because the monkeys took our cell phones," Eddie said.

My dad grinned and ruffled Eddie's hair. "Don't ever lose that great imagination you have!"

Eddie winked at me. Boy, he really had them fooled.

Eddie and I looked at the brochures. They were for summer camps; and not the boring kind. One had pictures of kids swimming in a big lake, arts and crafts, and horseback riding. I wanted to go there bad. Eddie's nose was glued to a brochure labeled *Space Camp*.

"Is this for real?" Eddie asked them.

"It is if you both keep up your grades and continue getting along," Allie said.

"You need to look through the brochures and pick one you both like," my dad said.

"Let us know which one you want. We want you two to have a fun summer, but we are not ready to let you go away from home for that long without each other. Josh, you're good at keeping Eddie on the straight and narrow," Allie said.

"And Eddie, you're good at helping Josh relax and enjoy himself," my dad added.

Our parents left looking quite happy. I could have sworn I saw them high-five each other outside our door. Did they want to get rid of us for a while? Maybe. But who cares? We were going to summer camp!

"Eddie, look at this camp." I said pointing to the canoes, the ropes course, and archery.

"So what? I want to go to Space Camp," Eddie said.

"But this one has a big bonfire and ghost stories, real ones!" I added.

"But if we go to Space Camp, I'll finally get the proof I need that Aliens landed on the moon."

"And how would you do that?"

"Duh, when we tour the moon."

"Eddie, just because you get to go to Space Camp, doesn't mean you actually get to go into space."

"I beg to differ, Josh. I heard this underground podcast from a kid who went to Space Camp. He shared very detailed information about touring the moon and finding old alien ruins."

"Ugh! We are not going to Space Camp!"

"I say we are!"

"No, we are not!"

"Yes, we are and I'm going to convince all our friends to go too," he said and crossed his arms defiantly.

"Listen, Mom and Dad said we had to pick one camp. One, Eddie. And Space Camp is not the one. Don't you want to go to a real camp where you can swim and kayak and ride horses?"

"That does sounds tempting, but I have to find out the truth. It's out there, Josh. I just have to dig it up and expose it to the world."

"You know we'll never agree." I said, and got a huge grin on my face.

"A series of dares to decide?" he grinned back and I nodded my head *yes.*

ABOUT THE AUTHOR

This book was written by the Nardini Sisters. Lisa lives in Florida and Gina Nardini-Christoffel lives in North Carolina. Although the sisters live in two different states, they still make time to write together. While growing up in the Ozarks, Lisa collected horse statues and Gina collected deer statues. Neither sister collected monkey statues.

The Underwear Dare was their first novel. *Zoo'd* is the second in the series. The Nardini Sisters are currently working on the third novel in the series featuring the same cast of characters as they venture into seventh grade.

The Nardini Sisters also have a collection of short stories co-written with their youngest sister, Sucia, and her daughter, Marina. It's called *HALLOTWEEN* and consists of 13 scary stories for tweens.

Visit their website at:
www.nardinisisters.com

Made in the USA
San Bernardino, CA
16 January 2014